MW01131433

Chosen Three

Hidden Secrets Saga, Volume 6

W.J. May

Published by Dark Shadow Publishing, 2015.

This is a work of fiction. Similarities to real people, places, or events are entirely coincidental.

CHOSEN THREE

First edition. December 5, 2015.

Copyright © 2015 W.J. May.

Written by W.J. May.

Also by W.J. May

Bit-Lit Series
Lost Vampire
Cost of Blood
Price of Death

Blood Red Series
Courage Runs Red
The Night Watch
Marked by Courage
Forever Night

Daughters of Darkness: Victoria's Journey
Victoria
Huntress
Coveted (A Vampire & Paranormal Romance)
Twisted

Hidden Secrets Saga
Seventh Mark - Part 1
Seventh Mark - Part 2
Marked By Destiny
Compelled
Fate's Intervention
Chosen Three

The Chronicles of Kerrigan
Rae of Hope
Dark Nebula
House of Cards
Royal Tea

Under Fire
End in Sight
Hidden Darkness
Twisted Together
Mark of Fate
Strength & Power
Last One Standing
Rae of Light

The Chronicles of Kerrigan Prequel
Christmas Before the Magic
Question the Darkness
Into the Darkness

The Hidden Secrets Saga
Seventh Mark (part 1 & 2)

The Senseless Series
Radium Halos
Radium Halos - Part 2
Nonsense

The X Files
Code X
Replica X

Standalone
Shadow of Doubt (Part 1 & 2)
Five Shades of Fantasy
Glow - A Young Adult Fantasy Sampler
Shadow of Doubt - Part 2
Four and a Half Shades of Fantasy
Full Moon
Dream Fighter

CHOSEN THREE

Hidden Secrets Saga
Book VI
By
W. J. May

Hidden Secrets Saga:

Download Seventh Mark part 1 For FREE
Seventh Mark part 2
Marked by Destiny
Compelled
Fate's Intervention
Chosen Three
<u>Book Trailer:</u>
http://www.youtube.com/watch?v=Y-_vVYC1gvo

Description:

How do you choose between life, love and the future?
You can't.
Rob's missing. Rouge's passed out.
Caleb just told her that Rob's been taken away to be put down.
Oh yeah, and Rouge's pregnant.
Wait, what?!
Rouge's the Seventh Mark, Michael's a guardian who's already dead. How can he get her pregnant?
The high and mighty Caleb is even more determined now to stop Rouge and the abomination growing in her belly.
On the run from Caleb and the Higher Council, on a mission to save Rob, and at the same time trying to stop the dark angel Rouge summoned – the team must figure out what the Power of Three is before Bentos kills them all.
However, there's a catch: if they go after the dark angel and kill it, anyone with angel blood in them will die. If they kill Bentos, there is rumor that all his offspring will die except the next Seventh Mark.
When everything looks lost, will there be any chance of hope for the future?
Find out in the final installment of the Hidden Secrets Saga, CHOOSEN THREE.
... or is it the final installment?

FIND W.J. May

Website: http://www.wanitamay.yolasite.com
Facebook: https://www.facebook.com/pages/Author-WJ-May-FAN-PAGE
Newsletter:
SIGN UP FOR W.J. May's Newsletter to find out about new releases, updates, cover reveals and even freebies!
http://eepurl.com/97aYf

Chapter 1

Time stood still with Grace's words.

"Rouge's pregnant with Michael's baby."

I closed my eyes and let the darkness take me, peace mine for the first time in a long time.

I might not be able to harm Caleb because of my love for Michael, but my duty to the child in my womb wouldn't settle for death.

The wind blew softly and each member of the fight before me slid through time as if a thick vat of plastic held them tightly in place. Darkness swam around me and my vision grew limited due to something inside of me sparking to life. I was born of light and darkness and where I preferred to act for the light, this time would be different.

I had no choice.

Bending slightly, I moved with expedience to shove my shoulder into Caleb's midsection. The force of my hit lifted him off the ground and sent him flying behind the group.

Voices slurred and words mingled in the plane which I found myself in, but it was irrelevant. My goal was to get Grace and Michael and go after my brother.

His death would lay waste to my desire to fight on the side of good anymore. It had never felt like my fight, and yet I was central to every moment of it since discovering my ancestral history.

I rushed the tall stranger-hunter holding Michael, spinning just before hitting him and pressing my back to his. I clipped my arm into his and let the trajectory of my movement force him away from Michael before he too was airborne.

Grace's brilliant blue gaze locked onto mine and I nodded, letting her know the moment was coming where she was going to have to decide.

Them or us.

The affirmation I saw left me breathless, my heart aching in my chest with realization. She and Michael, alongside my brother, were the family I'd been cheated of. They would stand beside me, protect me and help me put an end to all that we had endured in the name of goodness.

My right foot pressed hard against the earth as I bolted toward Sarah, my intent to force her back, but never hurt her. There had been far too much hurt in our world as of late. I wouldn't be a part of ushering in a new wave of it.

Grace lifted her hand and slammed her forearm into the side of Sarah's neck, throwing the beautiful woman off for a moment. I slid in behind her and locked my hands under her arms, pulling hard and twisting to throw her away from the center of the action.

A dull pain roared to life in the center of my stomach and I glanced back to see Michael as time finally sped up.

"We have to go. Now!" I took Grace's hand and ran toward the front of the house as Caleb's voice rose behind us. I wasn't interested in sticking around to watch his anger truly unfurl.

Michael jumped in the driver's seat of the black Bronco and hit the gas as the remaining hunters rounded the corner to the house.

"Hold on, girls. This is going to be rough for a minute." He turned off the paved road just outside of Caleb and Sarah's house and took to the thick woods. The headlights on the vehicle were kept off and we all sat in a tense silence as he expertly weaved us through the dense forest. Branches and leaves whipped against the SUV and the windows. The only noise was nature fighting against their destruction.

It felt like forever before the human silence was finally broken.

Michael's voice shook as he glanced in the rearview mirror at me and Grace. "You're pregnant, Rouge? Did he hurt you?" His brow furrowed as his tone thickened with what sounded like unshed tears.

"I don't know," I started but Grace reached out and squeezed my hand, giving me the look that said it was time to fess up. "I think I am... I'm pretty sure." I glanced down and brushed my fingers by my side, realizing that my shirt was coated in a thick crimson liquid.

"Crap! Are you bleeding?" Grace jerked back in the seat beside me and reached for the hem of my shirt, pulling it up and examining me though I slapped at her to get back. She would have none of my modesty.

"Do I need to pull over?" Michael asked.

"No!" Grace and I barked back in tandem.

"I'm fine. I probably fell on a stick or something when I dropped to the ground." I started to pull from her, but she held on tightly, her eyes going wide. "Plus, you can't stop. We need to get out of here."

"That's not a cut, Rouge! Your damn bone is sticking through the skin. Is this from Caleb hitting you?"

The pain of the wound reared to life as if her words gave it permission to spread its nasty sting throughout me. I gasped for a quick breath and sat back.

"What bone? What the hell are you seeing, Grace?" Michael was becoming frantic.

I gave Grace a look she completely ignored. Her concern was only for my well-being and I was grateful. I could feel myself slipping. I'd soon lose consciousness. "I'll be fine," I whispered roughly.

"No, you won't. We have to fix this. To get the rib back inside of you." Grace pushed at my shoulder. "Lean over and let me push it back in."

"Are you kidding me?" I glanced toward the window just beyond her and caught a glimpse of the moon.

Where's my brother? Please don't let him be hurt. Don't let him be taken from me.

Tears filled my eyes and I sniffled, not realizing what I was doing.

"Baby, don't cry. It's going to hurt like fire, but let Grace push the bone back inside of you. You're immortal like us now. You'll heal shortly, but that wound won't close properly with the bone sticking through it."

"What? I don't care about that. Just do it." I ground my teeth against each other and nodded as she pushed against my side.

Dizziness rushed across me as the pain exploded throughout my midsection. I cried out loudly and the vehicle swerved.

"Damn, Grace! Be careful with her." He watched me closely in the rearview mirror.

I nodded as Grace rubbed my shoulder. I would be fine, though my heart was broken over the situation with Rob. He'd saved me, kept me from being massacred in Florida and given up everything for me.

I'd put him in constant danger and delivered him straight to death. He would never trust me again, if there was an 'again' to have.

"I'm scared," I whispered, unable to keep the fear trapped inside me. I forced myself to sit up and take in long gulps of air.

"It's going to be okay. We'll figure this out like we always do—together." Grace moved closer and wrapped her arm loosely around my shoulders.

"Are you okay? Is the pain horrible?" Michael's voice was biting, but he too was scared. There had been far too much information flung at him for him to even begin to keep up.

"I'm okay. You?" I forced a tight smile and he shook his head, rolling his eyes.

I let the conversation die between us. We were both alive and that was saying a lot seeing that things weren't at all headed that way only moments before.

"What the hell did Caleb mean about us not being pure, Michael?" Grace's voice grated with mistrust.

"Why don't you come up here and I'll tell you what I know." Michael patted the seat beside him. "Let's let Rouge rest, and heal. We'll find shelter then figure out what our next steps are."

"I don't need to figure anything out." I offered Grace my hand to help her into the front seat, but she refused. I wrapped my arms around my waist, hugging myself tightly and leaning over to rest my head against the window in the backseat.

"What? Of course we do! Caleb'll be looking for us and I've no doubt your father too is after us." Michael let out an exasperated sigh. "I can't believe I just—we just—turned our back on him."

"Say goodbye to your understudy position," Grace added sarcastically.

"Yeah, well they can all rot in hell." I couldn't stop the anger from pouring out. "I'm going to find my brother. He deserves better than what I've let happen to him." My voice broke, but I closed my eyes tightly and tried to pull in the agony of letting Rob get taken.

Grace's hand tightened on my knee as she leaned back from the front seat. "It's not your fault."

"No? Whose is it then?" I spoke harshly, my adrenaline beginning to wane. I was left with a touch of the darkness that helped me survive only moments before. That deep evil that balanced out the good in the world lived in me like it did all of us. It just manifested in my life at times. Whether it was right or wrong was irrelevant. It just was.

"I guess if we're going to assign blame, then it's mine to carry." Michael hit his head softly on the headrest and growled. "Sanctuary was the promise. I can't believe Caleb went back on his word. He's broken the one truth we all live by and respect! I trusted him. I put up with his angry and unforgiving nature, but this?" He growled, nearly sounding like a Grollic. "Now he's set on killing Rouge? It's over. Whatever loyalty I had to him, is gone."

The pain in his voice brushed by me and I wanted to care, but I couldn't. Caleb was hell-bent on seeing light ushered into the world and the cost associated with such a grand scheme wasn't considered. So many people would be destroyed in his hunt for rightness and redemption, many of them never playing a part in the original game that started so long ago.

Michael would have to work out his acceptance of who Caleb was and the purposes for which he stood solidly by. I couldn't help with that, so I didn't try.

Closing my eyes, I let the world fade away and relived a few of the memories that would shape the next steps in my journey.

Learning of large covens of Grollics that weren't vicious, mindless beasts that everyone made them out to be really changed everything. Grollics were created by birth and many of these people never had a choice in the matter.

Where I knew my father had to die, the result of his death would be genocide to a race of animals who were innocent in most ways of the world. Just like any other race in the world, the Grollics had those that were bent toward evil and destruction, but for the most part they were no different than the hunters.

A group of people fighting for what they believed and willing to die to ensure tomorrow came, if not for them, then for those that would come for generations after.

The image of Joshua swept by my vision and I stifled a cry. Where I would never love anyone but Michael, Joshua had stolen a part of my soul. The Grollics believed in mates and he believed himself to be mine. I couldn't argue the point seeing that peace that surpassed comprehension was mine when he was there.

A tear dripped down my face as sadness rested in the center of my chest. Even at the end of his life he still pressed against my father's commands and tried to keep me safe. Good Grollics existed. Joshua had been one. My brother was another.

There had to be more, and what right did I have to take their lives by taking my father's? The war had to come to a close, but did all those that refused to participate willingly have to suffer finality because of it?

Grace's voice came out softly as it broke through my scattered thoughts. I shouldn't have listened, but I couldn't help myself.

"What did he mean, Michael?" Grace asked again. "You and I are full-blooded hunters. I refuse to believe anything else and yet the disgust on Caleb's face told us a different story." She hesitated and sucked in a long breath. "You're his understudy. Basically next to the throne! I don't get it."

Michael cleared his throat and spoke in a low voice. "There's a lot we don't know, Grace. We've simply been following Caleb's directives, which is what we were supposed to do. I've never asked about our father because the story I learned was that our mother was raped on her wedding day. You know. That's it. I accepted it, took me longer than you, but now, with some of the things I've seen lately..."

"What? What things?" Grace's voice lifted.

"Shhhh... Keep it down. I want Rouge to get some rest. I'm not sure what we'll find when we locate Rob and I want her to be levelheaded. Let her rest and keep your voice down to a dull roar, hmm?"

I laid silent in the back, wide awake and pretty sure Michael knew it, or he was in denial and wanted to believe I was sleeping.

"Shut up. Tell me what you saw that I didn't."

"I had a dream a few weeks back that was so real that it... it..." He paused and I forced my breathing to still. I needed to hear what he experienced. Michael would no doubt share the experience with me too.

"It what? Spit it out."

"Okay. Jeez... It felt real. I'm pretty sure it was real."

"Tell me about the dream."

"I was on the beach and this dark angel came and dug his claws in my back, toting me off into the distance. Rouge was there, but there was little fear if I remember it right. I'm not sure if she was scared, but I felt peaceful."

"A dark angel? That doesn't incite peace in me." She gave a sarcastic laugh.

"I agree, but I think he's a part of what Caleb was referring to. I don't like the situation and I hope I'm wrong, but I think he and I are connected."

"Connected? How?" Grace's voice rose in volume again.

"I don't know, and until I do, I'll be keeping the rest to myself." Michael coughed again. "I have far more questions than I have answers right now. I just want to get Rouge to safety and figure out what our next steps are."

"I'm so heartbroken over Caleb lying to us."

"I'm upset too, but he's a creature of habit, Grace. He was created to destroy the Grollics. We can't change that and we've been trying to."

"You're not seriously sticking up for him, are you?"

I flinched at the thought. Michael was insanely loyal to his mentor, but after all that had happened, Caleb wasn't a friend in the fight we were facing, but a dangerous foe.

"No. Not at all. I'm just stating the truth. You and I have to cut ties with him and Sarah or cut ties with Rouge. I'm not leaving her side, but if you feel like you have any loyalty left, you need to leave now. The lines have been drawn and we have to choose our side to stand on."

"I stand with you and her. Period."

"Good. I figured as much."

I covered my face as a fresh wave of tears washed down my cheeks. It wasn't a fight with only two opposing forces. Those of us who believed in inherent good capable of coming from both sides stood in the middle.

That was my place. Between the hunters and the Grollics.

I too would stand. Period.

Chapter 2

I must have dozed off, though I didn't remember doing so. Someone shook my shoulder softly, but didn't speak. I came to and sat up with a jolt. It had been the first sleep I'd had in months that wasn't filled with some kind of nightmare.

"Where are we?" I turned to find Grace standing outside of the car opposite of me.

"We're at a small cabin in the woods. In Oregon. Come on. Let's stop here for a while. Regroup and try to figure out where we're going from here." She gave a sad smile.

"Okay," I mumbled and moved gingerly from my warm spot in the Bronco, still feeling half asleep.

I expected the pain of my broken rib to take my breath away, but oddly I felt fine. Brushing my hands over my midsection as I got out of the SUV, I realized all was well. I had healed sometime during my nap.

"You okay?" Michael's voice caught me off-guard and I jerked around to see him.

"Yes. Just making sure my rib healed right." I continued to run my fingers over my side, but took note of the way his eyes watched me. Warmth spread from my chest up to cover my cheeks and burn me.

He smiled. "Why are you blushing?"

"Because," I barked. "I just am."

"I like it." He moved toward me, pulling me into a comfortable embrace. "You good?"

"Yeah, I think so." I rested against him as the darkened night echoed with life around us. "We need to find Rob. Fast. We have no time. They don't give a crap about his life."

"I know." Michael sounded upset by my last statement, which was huge. He was far more like Caleb in his being so mission-minded. Maybe things were changing. I could only hope.

"Come on, guys. You can snuggle inside, but it's cold out here." Grace opened the door to the quaint wooden cabin in front of us.

Sheesh, they have cabin's everywhere. "Whose is this?" I asked and pulled from Michael's arms. We had a lot to talk about in terms of the baby that lay inside of me, but I would bring it up later. My brother was the first order of business and far more important than me and Michael trying to work through whatever emotions would spring up from our situation.

"Don't know." Michael reached for my hand as we walked toward the cabin. "We're taking a chance with it. Grace picked it out of the dark as we were driving past. I doubt there's food or water, but it's shelter for a few hours. We won't stay long. Just long enough to figure out where we're going and hopefully clean you up."

Grace had disappeared into the darkness and as we approached, a light came on to illuminate what looked like a kitchen area. I moved inside and took a quick glance around. The kitchenette sat to my right, a two-seater table to my left and a living room beyond that. It was fully furnished, but looked as if no one had been there in ages.

"At least it has electricity and running water." Michael released my hand and walked toward Grace, who stood by the sink, checking the faucets. "Rouge, take off your top and come over here. Let's get you cleaned up."

I nodded and forced the angst inside of me to subside. Rob wasn't dead yet. I was as sure of that as I was the people standing in front of me. Something inside of me would have recognized

his death due to our connection. I could control all Grollics, but
with Rob it was almost automatic. I could feel his determination
to live. A smile brushed by my lips as the sound of him cursing
me filled up my head. He hated having me control him or anyone
else.

I hated it too most days, but it was a handy tool when needed.

"What're you thinking about?" Michael asked as I
approached.

Tugging my shirt off, I turned and gave him access to my side
where the rib had perforated the skin. "My brother being an ass."

"He's always an ass," Michael muttered and ran his fingers
over my side slowly.

"We're going after him, or at least I am. I can't let anything
happen to him. I just got him. He's all I have." I shivered and
turned to find Grace gone.

Michael glanced up, his dark blue eyes threatening to steal my
breath. "You have me, and Grace."

"Thank you." I wasn't sure what else to say, so I turned and
looked back toward the darkened house. "Where'd Grace go?"

"Probably to check for supplies."

A warm rag moved across my side slowly and chill-bumps rose
on my skin. I turned my attention back to Michael and reached
up, brushing my fingers by the side of his head.

"I love you." I didn't say it often because he knew, but after
everything that had happened, he needed to know.

He brushed the rag across me once more before tossing it
beside him and tugging me to rest in his arms again. His lips
pressed against the top of my head as I tightened my grip on him.

"I love you too." He stepped back just a bit, enough to give
space so he could talk. "Why didn't you tell me about the baby?"

Here it was. I knew the discussion would arrive far before I
was ready to handle it. "I wasn't sure if I actually was pregnant. I
didn't think it was possible." I cleared my throat. "I still have my
doubts." I glanced down at my slightly swollen stomach. "I

shouldn't though. Something's fluttering inside of me. I can feel it."

He ran the back of his fingers over my stomach as his breath caught. "Is this why you were so sick back at the hotel? Not just because of the Sioghra?"

"I guess so." I shrugged and pulled from him. "It might not matter anymore. I can't imagine a child surviving the transition from human to... to what I am. I had to die to become what I am now, right?" I was a hunter, I guess, but I was also a Grollic. What did that make me? A freak?

"Not human, but Grollic. You were different from the start of the transition. I guess that would make things even more complicated." He reached for me, but I swatted him away playfully.

"We can hold each other later. I need to find my brother." I picked up my torn shirt and slipped it back on my head. "Where's my journal?" Panic filled me. Had we left Bentos' journal back at the house in Port Coquitlam?

"In the backseat of the SUV. I grabbed your backpack as we raced off. I assume your journal is in there. I'll grab it." He moved past me, brushing his fingers along my arm as he did.

I turned and walked into the darkness, fear of such things long part of my past. After everything we had been through, the darkness was almost a welcomed reprieve more than anything else.

"Grace?" I called out to my friend and turned to walk down a short hallway that led to what I assumed to be a bedroom.

"Back here. There're a few t-shirts and socks in these drawers. I think they belonged to a man, but should be comfy, right?"

I walked in to see her holding up a worn Van Halen t-shirt with a big smile on her face.

"Yep. Looks like it will do the trick." I changed and grabbed a few more shirts before leaving with her to meet up with Michael.

He was leaning over the sink, drinking water from the faucet. Grace scolded him, but I ignored their banter. Finding Rob wouldn't be easy, but if anything could help me, I knew it would be my father's journal.

I dug through my bag and found it at the very bottom, next to the journal I'd bought to start transcribing the information for Caleb. That ship had sailed now. I wasn't doing anything for the head of the hunters. He was enemy number one, just beside my father from what I could gather.

"I'm going to step outside." I lifted the journal in the air.

"I'll come with you." Michael wiped his face on his shirt and moved toward me.

"No. Please don't. I need a minute to see if I can find Rob." I walked to the door, pausing only as Grace called out to me.

"Do you think he's still alive, Rouge? Can you feel him at all?"

"He's alive," I said tersely. "We'll find him. Just give me a minute to figure out how." I knew I sounded ticked, but they didn't know. They couldn't possibly understand my frustration. I shrugged as I tucked the journal against my chest and walked out into the chilly night air, maybe they did understand and I wasn't giving them enough credit.

An owl cried out in the distance, and where it once would have frightened me, it gave comfort now. It felt good to know I wasn't alone.

I found a large oak tree and pressed my back to it before sliding down to sit on the chilled ground below. The book grew warm in my hands, and that too was welcomed against the cold and dampness in the middle of the forest.

I flipped through the pages and found that even though it was too dark to see my hand in front of my face, the words glowed softly, making them easy to read.

So much of the information in the book had been locked away from me, but now most of it was open and readable. The wolf-speak, the language of my father's people, was something very few could read, but I could make it out as if it were plain English. From what everyone told me, I could speak it too, though I never could hear the difference when I did.

"Help me find Rob. Please." I flipped a few more pages and stopped at the picture of a bridge. It amazed me that I'd had this book and found things I hadn't seen before in it. I wondered if it might possibly be because I was looking at it in the dark.

Leaning over, I read what was written on the page. It took a few times rereading it but I was able to decipher the meaning. I read it out loud to clarify the information, "The one powerful enough to gain access to my words, has the ability to bridge the gap in space between where they are and where they want to be."

I brushed my fingers over the page as hope set in. The words moved slightly as if jolted by my touch and I smiled.

"Incredible." Such intense power should belong to no one, but I couldn't deny the draw it had on me. I knew without a doubt I would have to destroy the book once everything was said and done, but it would be a hard task to face. I was the only one capable of laying waste to the old magic which lay inside the leather bounds. It offered me protection, and knowledge. However, I knew I would have to burn it to protect myself. Not from others, but from the power inside of the words, the same power which had corrupted my father.

I couldn't take that chance. Not with the stark realization I would soon be a mother. *Seventh mark...*

"I can't handle that right now." I stood and pushed away the horror at being responsible for someone's well-being and mental stability. It was too much and not having a mother myself, I would be starting at a great disadvantage.

"Show me my brother. I want to be with him." I closed my eyes and pressed my hand to the page as the darkness turned to a blurry mix of yellows and reds.

The sound of a car passing by filled my ears, but it was in my vision, not reality. Rob was on the floorboard of a van, lost to a fitful sleep. His cries accompanied his arms jerking or legs twitching as if his dreams terrorized him.

"You're okay," I whispered and tried to look around the van to see who might have him. Two dark figures sat at the front, but I couldn't make them out. I pressed against the vision, trying to shift myself in the front with them, but it wasn't happening.

As long as Rebekah wasn't one of the ones in the front seat I would be fine. To think about killing her was almost too much to consider. I didn't think of her as my mother, but she was, regardless of how I felt about it. And she was Rob's mom.

Pulling back, I let out an aggravated sigh. "Where is he? That didn't help much other than to confirm that he's alive."

A gasp ripped from my lips as I jolted, the back of my head banging against the bark of the tree trunk. A bright beacon appeared in the sky almost like heaven had sent down a fiery bolt to hit someone. I rubbed my head. Was Rob at the end of the light?

It was too far away to tell where it landed, but the subtle shifting of it to my right told me that whatever it was tracking, the thing was on the move.

It had to be Rob.

I took off back toward the cabin and rushed into the house, half scaring Grace to death. If that was even possible.

"We have to go! Rob's in a van that's traveling sixty miles an hour or so. I can see him, but not who's got him." I grabbed my bag and shoved my journal back in it before turning on my friends and making my request a bit more urgent. "Let's go! I'm serious!"

"How do you know *where* we're going?" Michael asked, but moved to open the door for me.

"I can see a beacon in the sky where he is. We'll follow it, but we'll have to move faster than them if we're going to catch up." I jogged to the car and glanced back to catch Grace's attention. "You okay with me taking shotgun?"

"Of course." She bit at her lip and moved to get into the back. "Is he okay? He's not hurt too bad or anything, right?"

Michael had gotten in the driver's seat and slammed the door as Grace asked her questions. He glanced back at her and gave a sardonic huff. "She hasn't seen Rob, Grace. She just knows where he is."

I buckled up and nodded toward Michael. "Hit the gas, we gotta go. We're heading southeast. I'll tell you if that changes."

Grace's fingers brushed by the back of my shoulder and I reached up, trapping them against me. "He's okay. I saw him asleep in the back of the van. I don't sense anything life threatening yet." I had no idea if I could be sure on that, but it didn't hurt to hope and say the words out loud.

"Who has him?" Grace turned to Michael. "You know Caleb better than anybody. Who would he send to take Rob?"

"I don't know." The frown on Michael's face deepened. "I don't know Caleb as well as I thought I did."

"Where could they be taking him?" Grace's voice carried a layer of panic in it.

"It's hunters. I assume they're headed for Salt Lake City. We have a facility there, but why they're keeping him alive..." Michael turned on the heater and glanced over at me as I growled softly. "Sorry. I'm just saying."

"Yeah, well, don't. He's *my* brother." I turned to look out the window as tears burned my gaze. I was beyond tired, exhausted from the past few weeks and pregnant. I was starting to get scared. How long did we have before our journey ended with my brother's death slamming into the center of me?

Michael's hand brushed over my arm and squeezed softly. I patted his fingers and returned my gaze to the burning light out the front of our window.

Finding Rob wasn't the issue, saving him was.

Chapter 3

"We're getting closer. Drive faster." I sat up and pressed my hands to the dash, my heart racing inside of my chest.

"I'm going over a hundred, Rouge. We'll be lucky if I don't roll this thing over." His tone was demeaning, though I knew he didn't mean for it to be. He was tired and most likely broken up over everything that had happened with Caleb. The man was like a father to Michael and Grace.

Too bad their real father is a scary-ass monster.

"Drive faster," Grace barked from the backseat.

I wanted to thank her, but I left my thoughts unspoken. Michael was on edge. We all were. There was going to be a horrific fight on our hands by the time we reached my brother.

"How long have we been driving? Where are we?" I turned to my boyfriend and reached out, squeezing the thick muscle of his thigh.

"Hours. Probably five. We're three hours away from the facility from what I can tell on my phone. They have to stop for gas or food sometime soon. Can you see Rob still? Is it like an all-the-time thing when you close your eyes or what?"

"It's like astral projection. I can force myself into the back of the van with him, but I'm worried about doing it too often." I pressed my fingers to my face and rubbed softly. Weariness had set in a few hours back and I was sure I'd dozed off again.

"Does it leave you feeling weak?" He glanced over at me. "We don't want it to hurt the baby."

I glanced down and rubbed my hands over my stomach. It wasn't obvious I was sporting a baby bump unless someone knew what they were looking for. Even then, you couldn't tell. "It does make me a little tired." I tried to brush it off as not effective enough to hurt anything inside of me.

"Then don't do it again." Michael reached out and pressed his hand to my stomach as I glanced up at him. "You sure know how to create distractions to avoid talking about the serious stuff." He winked at me. "When we get Rob back, you and I are having a sit-down conversation."

"Okay." I smiled and covered his hand with mine. "I'll be careful, I promise. But I'm probably going to need to peek in on them to see where they are. The beacon is still as bright as it was during the night and definitely a lot closer."

Grace yawned in the backseat loudly. "Can we please make a restroom stop? I'm starving and need to go."

"Sure." Michael took his hand back and pulled into the next convenience store we saw.

Grace hopped out and I followed her into the store with Michael right behind me. He and Grace went to the restroom while I waited in the small hall outside.

I pressed my back to a rack of cans and closed my eyes, willing myself back into the van with Rob. He was sitting up, his knees bent and head pressed to his hands. From the slump of his posture I could tell that he had given himself over to defeat.

"I'm coming," I whispered, not at all expecting him to respond, but he did.

His head jerked up and eyes went wide. He moved to his knees and reached out toward me.

"Jamie? What're you doing here?" His voice was nothing more than a whisper, and his eyes darted back and forth between the front seat and me.

"I'm coming for you. We've almost caught up. Where are you?" I glanced toward the front, getting more than I did the night before. The guy driving wasn't someone I knew, but the woman sitting in the passenger-side seat was Rebekah.

No!!!!! Anger burned through me and I jerked my attention back to Rob.

"We're headed for Salt Lake City." Rob moved back to his seated position and put his head in his hands as a male in the front seat jerked around. I didn't recognize him.

"Who are you talking to, mutt?"

Rob ignored him and I jerked back, scared that he might see me like Rob had, but he glared at my brother for a split second and turned back around.

Sadness rolled over me at the fact that our mother hadn't said anything in Rob's defense. It was bad enough that the hunters had my brother and were carrying him to his death, but to know that our mother was intimately involved was horrifying. I couldn't wrap my head around the fact that she might be responsible for this. What the heck was her connection to Caleb? Or was there even one?

Was Rebekah not really Rob's mother? Maybe she was just someone who took care of him when he was younger. He was a Grollic. Bentos had a habit of killing off his children, what about a wife or two as well?

Rob moved and my vision focused back on him. "We'll be there in a couple hours. That's what the GPS is reading. Hurry. I'm going to fight like hell, but I'm outnumbered already and it's only going to get worse." He looked up from his hands at me as a smile played on his lips. "I knew you would come."

"I'll always come for you, just like you would for me. We're trying to catch up. Hold on and keep fighting till we get there." I wanted to reach out and steal a warm hug from him, but I was nothing more than a ghost in the midst of his tribulation. I pulled back and let out a cry as Michael walked from the bathroom.

"Rouge. What's the matter?" He took me by the arms and half held me up as my knees threatened to buckle.

Large tears dripped down my cheeks and it was suddenly so hard to breathe. I reached for him and wrapped my arms around his neck, pressing my face against his shoulder.

"Are you in pain, Rouge?" His voice was all business. He sounded like Caleb.

"No." I managed to get out one word before a soft sob left me. The situation with my brother was horrifying, but the heartbreaking part was that the woman he believed to have birthed him, to have loved him like no other was part of his coming death. Why?

"Hey, what's going on?" Grace moved up beside me and put her face in mine. "Is something wrong with Rob?"

"He's alive," I mumbled and pulled back before wiping at my tears. "They're a couple of hours away from the facility. We need to hurry."

"Why are you so upset?" Michael glanced between me and Grace and held up his hands in a show of surrender. "I mean, beyond the obvious reasons."

"Rebekah's in the passenger seat."

"What the hell?"

I understood Michael's confusion all too clearly. "It breaks my heart... for my brother." I shook my head and turned, disappearing in the restroom and leaving Grace and Michael to work the rest out. Their story wasn't much different from mine or Rob's, but having Sarah and Caleb there to raise them had to help out a little. Rob had Rebekah, but I had no one.

I almost felt like I was in the better position because of it. Caleb had sunk his knife in deep with Grace and Michael back at his house. His deceit over promising sanctuary and then attacking us the minute we got there had to hurt deeply.

My brother felt the same level of hurt, no doubt. A shudder ran through me, but I forced my thoughts away and worked to wash my hands and my face before rejoining my companions.

After picking up a few bags of chips, some powdered donuts and a soda, I was back in the SUV with Grace and Michael and ready to hit the road.

"You know we're going to have another fight on our hands when we get there," Grace mumbled from the backseat between bites of her corn chips.

"It should be on a lesser scale this time." Michael sat up straight, his attention on the rearview mirror. "There should be four or five hunters there, but none of them will be as strong as Sarah or Caleb. Let's just pray they aren't there."

"Yeah. I'm not at all ready to see them." Grace was hurt, and she should be.

"We need to try to find a place to hide the car and go in on foot." I glanced toward Michael. "Waltzing in there like we own the place is going to get all of us killed."

"There is no 'going in on foot', Rouge. The facility sits on a cleared three-acre plot of land. We'll be driving right up to the front door. All I can tell you two is that you need to be ready to fight. We'll get inside because I'll run through the gates and hit the door with the vehicle. After I do, we get out and Grace and I will rush whoever is in the main hall on guard. Rouge, you find Rob and once you do, get back to the car and we'll join you shortly."

"I don't think she should go in at all. She's pregnant." Grace leaned up in the front seat and smiled at me as I glared at her.

"I'm not sitting in here while you two put your lives on the line for my brother." I shook my head. "It's not happening."

"Michael. Tell her. Seriously. It's not safe." Grace poked at her brother.

He swatted her hand back. "Stop that. I'm driving."

"Tell her," Grace urged him.

Michael glanced toward me and I gave him my best, 'you better not' look. He swallowed and shrugged.

"I'm not telling her anything. She's capable of bringing down the whole place on her own. We're all needed." He took a long drink of his coke as Grace huffed and flung herself back in her seat.

"You really think I can bring the whole place down?" I turned my attention to Michael as his words sparked something to life inside of me.

"Yes. You're the seventh son of the seventh son and a hunter. I honestly think your father had it right. You're beyond important to this fight we have coming up. It's going to be you that wins it for us, and where that scares me to death... it excites me too." He glanced over at me and reached for my hand, pulling it to his lips and kissing my fingers softly.

I tugged my hand from him, not wanting to feel the foreign feelings of lust that lay deep inside of me. Now wasn't the time, and too many battles lay before us to relax into a life well-deserved just yet. The war was still looming in the distance and where I found truth in Michael's words, I still didn't understand it.

Up to that point I'd done well against Grollics and the hunters, but in the fights with my father, I'd lost over and over again. He was beyond powerful and evil incarnate. How many more chances would I get to try again?

None. This next time would be my last. Finality sat heavy on me, but a spark of recognition lay inside my chest. I would win this next time. I was ready... I just needed to figure out what the power of three was and gain the final objects. With those beside me and my friends at my back, we would win this thing.

"I have a question." Grace's voice lacked depth, as if her thoughts had carried her far off, much like mine had me.

"What?" Michael's tone was flat, monotone.

"After this, I assume we're going after Bentos."

"What seems like the right next step?" Michael glanced back up in the small mirror and nodded.

I decided to stay out of their conversation for a minute to see where it would lead to.

"If Rouge kills Bentos, then won't all Grollics die?"

Pain filled my chest at the thought of annihilating a race of beings that everyone thought deserved the sting of death, but me. I knew there were good ones. It was so incredibly unfair.

"I do believe that's how it happens." Michael looked over at me. "Do you know the answer to her question?"

"No," I whispered and turned to look out the window as the sun sat high in the sky. "I'm hoping we figure out a different way around it all by the time our next fight comes."

"The Grollics have to die, Rouge. They're beasts."

I looked back at him and shook my head. "No, they're shifters, which leaves them half human too. You're not different from them. You don't belong here where the humans rule and reign. I don't either."

"She has a point, plus, there are some really good ones just like there are some good hunters," Grace offered up.

"I would say that all hunters are good, but that's not the case at all, is it?" Michael sat back in his seat and pressed his fingers to his mouth.

All of us would have to go through the process of figuring out how to redefine good and evil. It wasn't so clear-cut as we'd thought it to be only six months back. Then it was easy. Grollics were beasts from hell and the hunters were angels from heaven, sent to fight back evil and save the day. Sort of. But not really either. But angels were considered good, right?

But now... Joshua and Rob had blown that theory out of the water, and Caleb and Sarah had muddied the truth. Who was right or wrong was almost irrelevant. The only purpose I had in mind was to remove true evil from our path, which would include my father and Michael's.

I reached over and took his hand, leaving our intertwined fingers in his lap and pressing my cheek to my shoulder.

He needed to know the truth of what I'd discovered. The dark angel was his and Grace's father. I wasn't sure what it all meant, but knowing something and keeping it from him left me feeling horrible.

"I'm not killing my father until I find out how to save my brother," I mumbled while watching the handsome boy who had stolen my heart and planted life in my belly.

He nodded and turned to watch me for a moment. "And if there is no saving anyone... then what?"

"I'm not ready to consider that just yet." I closed my eyes and took a deep breath. "Wake me up when we reach the facility. I'm so tired."

"Just rest. We'll figure this out piece by piece. This first one is to get Rob back. We'll do that and then figure out what's next. Stop rushing into the future. Stay with me here in the present."

I squeezed his hand and released it, clasping my own in my lap and letting the darkness take me. Michael was right. The future was far too frightening to try and traverse it alone. I needed him and Grace beside me, but I also needed my brother.

We're coming. Just hold on a little longer, Rob.

Chapter 4

"We're here." Michael tapped my leg, and I was instantly awake, the plethora of concerns racing through my brain having stolen any hopes of a deep rest.

"I'm up." I sat forward and glanced back at Grace who was busy biting her nails. "You okay?"

"Yeah. Just tired of fighting so much." She chuckled, but the sound lacked joy. "I guess that's the life of a hunter, 'eh?"

"We're all taking a serious vacation when this is over." I reached back and squeezed her knee. "In another country. And not Canada."

"Sign me up." She turned her attention to the view out of the front window. "There it is."

I jerked back around and leaned over, tucking my bag under the seat. "If anything happens to me, give my journals to Rob and if anything happens to both of us... destroy them. I don't want anyone having the information and you two would just be hunted down if you kept it with you."

"Nothing's going to happen to you. I won't let it." Michael hit the gas and pulled at my arm. "Get up and prepare for impact."

"Actually," Grace corrected him, "you need to relax. It'll hurt less if you slump down as if unaware of what's coming." She tapped my seat trying to get my attention.

I forced myself to relax, though everything inside of me screamed to get out of the car before it hit the building. At a ridiculously high speed, we approached the thin metal gate and

Michael barreled right through it, the SUV only picking up more speed and racing toward the large building before us.

"Oh crap!" I closed my eyes and covered my face, not able to watch us hit the large structure. Wrapping my hands around my stomach, I lifted up a prayer for safety for the baby inside of me if nothing else.

On impact I jerked forward, the seatbelt biting into my flesh as the sound of the crash filled the space around us.

"Everyone okay?" Michael's eyes were illuminated to a high blue, shining with supernatural power.

I nodded and scrambled to get out of the car.

"I'm good," Grace responded and moved by my side, stopping and glancing at Michael. "Maybe she should stay here. I'm serious."

I glared at her and poked my finger in her chest. "This is my fight and you're invited to help. Stop trying to protect me. I don't need you!"

She took a step back and nodded, my eyes having darkened no doubt. Everything had dimmed and yet I knew that my surroundings hadn't changed. Only I had.

I reached up and caught an arrow that whizzed past us before it hit Grace. "Let's go! Maybe you should stay back," I added sarcastically.

"Move fast with us." She grabbed my hand and we sped through the open floor of the large foyer in front of us.

Michael was right behind, but turned as we reached a long hallway. "I'll hold them off. Rob'll be in one of the rooms at the end of the hall. The rooms are charged with negative ions."

"What?" Grace paused momentarily in her movement.

"We—They—do that so it'll weaken you significantly. Go! But be careful." He looked as if he wanted to say something else, but turned and ran back into the main entrance as three hunters moved in on us, one still shooting poison-filled arrows.

"Help Michael," I hissed at Grace. "I'll get Rob."

She looked ready to protest.

"Don't let anything happen to Michael." I pushed her back into the main room and slammed the door behind her, locking it. The hallway ahead of me seemed too quiet compared to the noise on the other side of the door.

The grimace on Grace's face would have been comical had it been another time and another situation, but I ignored the thought and raced toward the rooms at the end of the hall.

Muffled voices caught my attention and the light beam I'd set in motion was almost vibrating on the last room. I pushed my legs harder and without hesitating, shoved my shoulder against the door, forcing it open and barreling in.

I jumped up instantly, crouched and ready to pounce.

Rob lay strapped with metal shanks to a stainless steel table. He turned in my direction, unable to lift his head or speak because of the metal-looking tape over his mouth.

A large, dark-skinned hunter beside him pinned me with a nasty stare, but didn't move toward me. "Good! We were hoping this would draw you out." He laughed and secured a shank on Rob's arm tighter, then moved toward me.

I stopped him, raising my hand to hold him from approaching momentarily as I glared at the other person in the room.

My mother. Rob's mother. Our betrayer.

The oppression of the magic in the room rolled over me, lifting every hair on my arms and the back of my neck to stand to attention.

"He's my brother. Family means something to *me*." I threw the insult toward Rebekah, but couldn't take my eyes off of the behemoth in front of me. He had already realized my hand didn't hold any magic to stop him. His strength alone was going to be a lot to contend with.

"Get out of the room, Jamie. It's got something that sucks your power..." Rob's words were slurred, his expression that of a drunk man. They'd drugged him. His own mother!

I wiggled my fingers and gave the hunter a 'come-hither' motion as I stepped back into the hall.

He shot toward me, punching and kicking in a succinct fashion, which was both impressive and terrifying. I backed up faster, ducked and twisted to keep from getting hit as best I could. There was no time to press an offense of my own. He wasn't allowing for that.

A growl escaped me as I realized that Rob was alone with our betraying mother in the room. I didn't want to take my eyes off of him and the jerk in front of me was causing me to do just that.

I spun around him, my tiny frame more agile than his massive one, just as he started his second wave of attack. As I moved, I kicked out hard. My heel planted into the back of one of his knees, forcing him to fall forward. I kicked again at his back, forcing him to fall face down on the tiled floor. The distinctive crack let me know I'd broken his nose and his forehead hit the ground hard. I popped my head into the room, trying to ensure my brother was okay and ready to kill my mother by any means necessary.

Shocked at the scene before me, I stopped momentarily.

Rebekah looked up with tears in her bright blue eyes. She was working to undo Rob's restraints. "Hurry!" she whispered.

What the h—I turned just in time to take a punch to the face that was sure to leave something broken. Crimson red dripped from my cheek as I ducked and pressed my shoulder into the large hunter, grunting and picking him up like I had Caleb the night before. I threw him across the hall with all of my might.

He dented a closed door behind him as he plowed into it and fell to the ground. A deep laugh left him and he stood, dusting off his shirt and cracking his neck. "Not bad for a little girl." He grabbed his crooked nose and straightened it like it was nothing.

"Little girl?" I pulled the darkness from the inside of me and held my hands out toward him. I was done fighting fair. He had brute strength and speed on his side, but I had power. True, dark, inherent power.

I spoke in a low tone, the words barely comprehensible as I let myself go and pressed darkness from the center of my palms out onto him.

He screamed and turned around, clawing at himself as if a thousand bees were stinging him. The horror of it pulled me from my protective stance and I slipped into the room with my brother and Rebekah.

"Shut the door. Now!" she screamed at me and I did it before pressing my forehead against it and trying to catch my breath.

If anyone would have seen me, they would have run from me. The look of horror on the hunter's face before I zapped him was unforgettable.

What the hell was that?

The same deep sense of evil, which had pressed against me back at Caleb's house, that had afforded me strength and speed, rolled over me then. Could the child in my womb be something completely different than I was? Had he taken on more of my father's nature than my own? Had the power come from the child?

"Rouge! We have to go. Now!" Rebekah grabbed my shoulder, jerking me from my position against the door.

"Don't touch me! You're involved in this," I hissed as I pressed a finger into her chest and gave her an accusing glare.

"No! Never! I'm here to help." She turned and hurried back to Rob. "I'll tote him, just clear the way. Is Michael with you?"

I shook my head, forcing the need to blast her with a round of darkness too. I couldn't do it though, with Rob unable to move, I would need the help to get Rob to safety.

"Fine." I opened the door and moved out into the hall, ready to throw a few punches of my own. The male hunter was on the ground, still and surrounded by a puddle of dark liquid.

"What happened?" Rebekah spoke just beside me.

I ignored the question. "Let's go." I hurried down the hall, cautious and ready as we passed each closed door. Terrified and ready to kill if another hunter should jump out. Rebekah raced as fast as she could behind me half carrying, half dragging Rob. How she was able to hold his heavy muscular weight wasn't a question I had time to ponder.

At the end of the hall I unlocked the door to the main entrance. Michael and Grace stood fighting off two hunters each. It would be so easy to lift my hands and press darkness on the other hunters attacking my friends, but I knew better.

There was no way of making sure that my darkness didn't touch Michael and Grace and if it didn't, and it saved them, what would they think of me? I was tired of running and yet fighting meant letting a part of me come alive that was dark and destructive.

I glanced behind at Rebekah. "Take him to the SUV and if you hurt him or threaten any of us, I'll kill you."

Sadness brushed across her features, but I didn't have time for sympathy. She wasn't on my side and that meant she was against me. "Where's the SUV?"

"You won't miss it."

She nodded and moved along the far right wall with Rob. I couldn't believe I was trusting her with my brother. If she took off with him, I'd kill her with my bare hands, there'd be no need for dark magic. Throwing my shoulder back, I wiped my cheek that had already healed and I joined Grace. She took one hunter and I stepped in to fight a female hunter just standing up after Grace had tossed her against the wall. She moved back to Grace and I stepped in her path, flipping her onto the ground, keeping a tight grasp around her neck. I pressed my hand to her throat. Murmuring quietly, I imagined Grollic venom seeping out of my fingernails and into the skin of her neck. Shocked, I watched the light in her eyes go out as she struggled against me.

It was us or them, and I couldn't fathom losing anyone else.

An arrow whizzed past me as I stood, it ripped my shirt on my shoulder. My eyes darted over to the guy who kept shooting the damn things.

"No Rouge! They're poisonous!" Michael screamed, but I ignored him and ran toward the guy as he shot off another arrow. He was on the other side of the freakin' big lobby.

Rebekah, appearing out of nowhere, jumped in front of me as the male forwent his arrows and brought out a gun, firing it three times and hitting my mother in the chest. She spun around and smiled at me as the light in her eyes dimmed.

"No!" I screamed as terror and realization laced through me. She hadn't been there to harm us, but to help! She had to have been there the whole time to keep Rob safe from Caleb. It was she who had fought back against my father. She had given up everything for me and Rob.

Understanding choked me as I reached for her, catching her just before she fell. Michael attacked the hunter as I dropped to the ground with Rebekah.

"I'm sorry," she whispered as her eyes flickered again, the light growing dim. "I only wanted to save you and Rob."

"I'm so sorry." I pulled her close to me, hugging her tightly as I stifled the scream that beat against my chest. What had I done?

"I love you, Jamie. Tell Rob that I..." She choked and her eyes fluttered closed as she died in my arms.

"No... No... Please no! Don't leave us. I didn't know. I thought..." I glanced up to see Michael pinned to a wall and Grace taking a hard punch in the jaw.

Agony split me in half and I screamed from the depths of my soul, the building shaking violently around us as I let the wail out.

The darkness that welled up inside of me spilled out of my mouth and rushed around the room, wrapping each of those opposing us in a dark cloud that twisted and turned until they fell silent.

A hand pressed on my shoulder as I collapsed around my mother, holding her tightly and crying against her chest.

"Jamie! We have to go. Let me help you." My brother picked me up and forced my arm over his broad shoulders as he moved us back to the SUV.

I was numb. Powerless to stop the tears or pain breaking my heart. Unable to stop myself, I looked back at the destruction I had caused. My mother was dead in the middle of her people and that was my fault too.

Michael's eyes were brilliant blue, wider than I had ever seen them as he jogged up beside me, moving to take Rob's place. Rob released me and went to Grace as we ran to the now useless SUV stuck half inside the building. "Outside," Michael barked.

We followed him, my mind blank as he lifted my feet off the ground to run faster. Another black company SUV sat parked in the lot, probably from more hunters coming to help attack us.

The driver, whoever it had been, hadn't bothered to take the keys out of the ignition. We piled back into the car, an exact replica of the one we had just been driving in.

I slumped down in my seat and closed my eyes, trying to force the horror of my own actions from my thoughts. I wanted to fight for good, to be anything but a murderer like my father was, and yet life wouldn't afford me the chance. It was us or them, and I had to keep choosing. I hated it.

"No. Shit!" Michael got back out of the car and glanced over to me as I jerked up.

"What?" There was no time to concern myself with what I'd done or who I was becoming. Fight or flight. We sure as hell couldn't run away at the moment. A large group of hunters moved around the gated area as if they'd appeared out of nowhere. *Probably from the SUV we'd just jumped in.*

"I thought there were only a few of them," Grace muttered.

I got out of the car, as did Rob and Grace.

"There's a hidden facility underground, but I thought it was abandoned. I guess I was wrong." Michael slid his hand through his hair. "We're not going to make it out of this alive."

There had to be twenty of them and only four of us, Rob was weak and we were beyond exhausted.

They began to move our way, like an army all in perfect step. Their blue eyes all bright and angry.

Suddenly they stopped in unison as a pretty blond hunter stepped forward and lifted her hand. She turned her gaze specifically on me and smirked. "The four of you have to die for what you've done. You can go fast and painless or we can fight until you weaken, but either way you'll die. Caleb's on his way. This ends here. Today."

I glanced toward Michael as Grace moved beside her brother and leaned forward, speaking directly to me. "Do what you did back there. Let that darkness out again."

I shook my head. "I don't think I can."

"You can do it."

I closed my eyes and tried to summon the anger and darkness. I lifted my hands, palms upward trying to gather whatever I could inside of me.

Nothing happened.

I gasped and tried again.

Nothing.

"No!" I whispered and opened my eyes. "I can't, Grace."

She nodded and smiled, slipping her arm around Michael's shoulder. "Then we fight like hell. If we die, we go out on our terms, not theirs! Let's go out with a bang, shall we?"

Rob moved closer beside me. "I'm so sick of this shit! I'm ready too. Let's do this." He growled deep in his chest, his body vibrating, readying to shift.

"No," I whispered and moved away from him, walking to the back of the vehicle and letting out a shaky breath. There was one thing I could do.

I would have to bring in Michael's father, Malaz, to decimate everyone in front of us. It was my only choice.

I clenched my hands into fists. I had to hope like hell he wouldn't turn his dark power on us and kill us too.

"What're you doing, Rouge?" Michael moved beside me as the blond huntress began laughing.

She called out, able to hear us clearly with her hunter powers. "She's running out of options, twin hunter." She clicked her tongue against her teeth. "Such a disappointment, by the way. We had high hopes for you and your sister. Caleb's going to be sooo disappointed." The sarcasm dripped from her voice on her last sentence.

I ignored her bantering, knowing it was a ploy to get us to rush at them. I closed my eyes, preparing to call the dark angel. It was only a moment before I whispered his name that everything changed.

My eyes popped opened by the sudden confusion. Chaos was taking place among the hunters.

"What's happening?" Michael grabbed me and pulled me back into the building where Rob and Grace had raced ahead of us.

The hunters ran around, beating each other furiously as if madness had taken hold of them.

"Are you doing this?" Rob turned to me with horror on his face.

It was a look I never wanted to see again.

"No!" I jerked from Michael. I forced my legs to walk outside again. I was terrified to the core of my being.

Who was doing this? I shook with uncontrollable fear.

A smile lifted from the perpetrators mouth as he stood a mere twenty feet from me, his hands lifted and his eyes completely black.

I gasped.

Bentos.

My father.

Chapter 5

Grace's screams were muted due to the loud wind that blew around us. I moved forward, not paying attention to the hunters as they ran about frantic beside me. I assumed Michael and Rob were with Grace, helping to take care of whatever was wrong with her.

A moment in front of my father was one I wanted, but not quite yet.

"I felt your power only moments ago. Brilliant," he whispered reverently as his dark hair moved about his shoulders due to the strong breeze around us.

"I hate you!" I hissed in a quiet voice, sounding more calm than I felt. "You'll die for all you've done."

"We all die, Rouge. Immortality is a lie and one we've all bought into." He tilted his head to the side and studied me with his dark eyes. "Did you kill Rebekah? Oh... you did." He tutted.

I shuddered at the thought of him being able to pry into the memories inside of my head. If I ever doubted his power, my wayward thinking was righted in that moment. "She died trying to save me," I pointed out, not really believing the fault belonged to anyone but me. I hadn't cared what happened to her moments before her death, I was too angry at the lies and the hidden secrets that had plagued my life. My heart ached now at the idea of her sacrifice. Whether it was for me or Rob, or both of us, it didn't matter. She laid down her life once again for us, and my parting words to her had been incredibly harsh. Words my father would have said, not words I should have uttered. I'd spend the rest of my short life trying to fix my wrongs.

"So many people have already died and will continue to die for you." He shrugged and took a menacing step toward me. "Is it all worth it, my dear Rouge? To bring death and darkness to so many people?"

I had no answer for him. Nothing was worth the loss of life of others for me. Nor was it worth what I had suffered, nor would undoubtedly continue to. My life was worth nothing, and yet everyone around me believed different. Except Caleb. Maybe he was right in his thinking.

I glanced behind me and caught Michael's gaze.

Fear sat on his features, the grimace on his mouth not at all belonging to him.

I jerked back around and growled at Bentos. "Let him go. This is between you and me."

"No, child. It's between us and them, I know the future enough to realize that you have chosen a different path to walk. I killed you in the woods and you sent the angel to do your bidding." He shook his head as if disappointed. "He requires a price, but I'm sure you found that out moments ago, hmmm?"

"The darkness?" I muttered as Grace screamed again. Was the darkness that poured from me related to my Grollic inheritance or because of entangling myself with the Michael's father? Something told me the latter rang true.

"Save your brother if you can." Bentos smiled as a chill ran down my chest. "Today is not the day you die."

"I won't thank you for your help." I took a step back, ready to turn and see what was wrong with Rob, but unable to let my father out of sight for too long. He would most likely take complete advantage of us all if I did.

"No need for thanks. I didn't come to offer aid, but to protect something that means a great deal to me." He smirked and took a step back. "You will die soon, child, but these hunters won't get to celebrate that victory. It belongs to me and me alone."

He moved far too quickly for my eyes to make sense of where he went. I let out a sharp exhale and turned as the wind died down. Carnage lay all around us, the hunters who had gathered being brutally murdered without ever feeling the sting of a weapon.

Grace glanced up from beside the car, tears streaming down her face as she yelled for me again. "Rouge! Get over here. Rob's not breathing." She held my brother tightly in her arms and it took a few tries to get her to back off of him, but with Michael's help, I finally had unrestrained access to Rob.

His eyes were glossy, but opened, the beautiful amber having dulled significantly.

I leaned over and pressed my ear close to his mouth, listening for signs of him breathing and getting nothing. Grace screamed again and I glared up at her and Michael.

"Get her away from us until I can figure this out."

He nodded and dragged his sister back into the building behind them, the girl hysterical as she kicked and screamed the whole way.

A calmness settled over me that didn't make sense, but I wouldn't deny my gratefulness for it. Rob was going to make it through all of this with me. I just knew it.

"Breathe, dammit." I pressed on his chest, starting CPR. Leaning over, I forced air from my lungs down into his chest and then moved to repeat my sequence on his chest.

It took six times of moving back and forth between offering Rob the air from my lungs and beating on his chest for him to come to.

He jolted up and sucked in a deep breath before looking around wildly.

I didn't give him much time to get his bearings before I wrapped him in a tight hug and let out a sob. Fear rushed in and destroyed the peace I held onto for as long as possible.

Rob wrapped his arms around me and held me tightly as he shook slightly. "What the hell happened?"

"Dad showed up and poured darkness all over this place. I guess it affected you, though it shouldn't have." I moved back and ran my hands down the side of my brother's face, making sure he looked well enough to stand before getting up myself.

He took my offered assistance and stood, reaching out and propping himself up with the side of the SUV. "Where's Grace?"

I bit back the tears threatening to fall. "Get in the car. We need to get out of here." I looked around as bile rose up in my throat. There were far too many lives lost and yet it would have been us lying lifeless on the ground if Bentos hadn't shown up. "I'll get Grace and Michael."

I wanted to owe him nothing, although the truth was that I owed him everything in that moment.

Michael emerged from the building with my backpack over his shoulder. He helped Grace into the backseat. She moved quickly to help my brother get in beside her. She pulled him into her arms and cuddled his head against her chest.

"I'm thinking whatever just happened might well be worth it." He forced a chuckle that fell flat.

I climbed in the front and looked at Michael. "Get us out of here, now."

"You got it. Caleb'll be here any minute." Michael put the SUV in reverse and hit the gas, jerking us backwards as he spun the wheel.

I gritted my teeth and held on to the door handle as we swung around only to take off again toward the exit.

"Let's get on the road and we'll figure all of this out after everyone's had a moment or two to chill out." Michael reached over and took my hand. "I don't even know what to s..."

I cut him off. "Don't. I'm not in the mood to answer a million questions that I don't have the answer to. I've no clue what happened back there." I gritted my teeth and faced forward, not even Michael able to calm the terror building inside of me. "I'm working at not falling apart."

I didn't want to hear his lecture on me being evil or dark and having to work all of that out of me. I didn't need to analyze anything just yet, because the answers were simply too frightening and I was too fragile.

"I was just going to thank you, Rouge. You saved all of us. Unconventional way of doing it, but we're safe. Grace and your brother are alive and the baby's okay. Right?" He glanced toward my stomach and back to my face.

My peripheral vision showed me his actions. "I think so. I feel fine. Besides, well, exhausted. Confused. Horribly sad, but fine." I squeezed his hand and rested my head against the back of the seat as I let out a long sigh.

Grace's hushed tones lulled me toward my weariness. She was talking to Rob about how much she cared about him, how scared she was that something happened, and how she would protect him until he was strong enough to do it himself.

Gratefulness swam in the pit of my stomach and I lifted Michael's hand to my face, pressing my cheek to it and closing my eyes.

"It's okay, baby. We're all okay. I'm right here." His voice was soft and far more caring than I had heard him be in a while.

I nodded, not trusting myself to say anything without letting the waterworks go. There was no time for crying, plain and simple.

My father was playing a game with all of us, one that I couldn't deny anymore. We weren't in search of him at all. He was tracking us. We would find him and have our final showdown the minute he was ready and not a moment before. I wasn't in control, nor did I have the upper hand.

He did.

I huffed in frustration.

He always did.

"Rouge." Michael's voice shook me out of my desolated thoughts. "Caleb's going to have to clean up the mess at the facility before he begins tracking us. He can't afford to leave that massacre just lying there. The Higher Coven is going to have questions for him."

I stared blankly at him, no idea what he was trying to tell me.

"We can stop somewhere for the night and get back on the road tomorrow." Michael handed me his phone. "We need to stop. I need to rest. I haven't slept in two days. I can't keep going like this and be on top of my game." He shifted, his body sore from the beatings he'd taken. "We'll be useless against Caleb, Bentos, or whoever, if we don't."

"Okay." Was he asking me for permission or just telling me as a courtesy? Why hadn't he asked Grace or Rob what they thought? I glanced back at my brother, his arm around Grace as he dozed against the window. He looked exhausted.

Why had he collapsed? Had he come back to life because of the CPR? I knew one thing for sure: he was dead when I got to him, and the chilled feel of his skin made me realize now that he must have slipped off at Grace's first scream. That was why she had been hysterical.

If his heart had stopped then he'd died. I shook my head. Too much terror and information in one short period. If Rob had died and come back, was he half hunter? Could he be like me? How was that possible? None of it made sense.

Except, the answer was a logical one. Rebekah was his mother and like me. If he'd died, he would go through the internal transformation soon.

"Can we get something to eat? Being kidnapped, beaten and nearly dying is tough business." Rob coughed and lifted his head off the back of the seat.

"Yeah. I'll drive through somewhere." Michael glanced at my brother in the rearview mirror. "Want anything in particular?"

"Rouge, you hungry for anything?" Rob asked me.

"I don't care." I shrugged. I needed to eat but it didn't matter what. Just fuel. My stomach hadn't been ill for the last day or so, but it was most likely do to the high level of adrenaline that pumped through me because of our race against time.

"I'm going with a burger, six please." Rob sat back.

"Six burgers? You're such an animal." Grace laughed and propped her feet up between me and Michael.

Rob ignored her banter, which was far out of character for him. It had to be because he was simply exhausted, like the rest of us.

Worry rose in my chest over where Rob's thoughts were. He had to be scared of what happened to me back at the warehouse, of what I was capable of. I was scared, and if that was the case, then Michael was terrified too. Shoot we all were, including me.

I flipped on the light above my brother and Grace, illuminating the darkening car.

"What's that for?" Rob covered his face with his hand and growled at me.

"How're you feeling?" I pushed at his hand and took his chin into my grasp, forcing him to look up at me.

His amber eyes were full of fire once again, but showed no signs of blue.

It didn't make sense. He had to belong to Bentos and Rebekah just as I did, and yet he hadn't gone through the transition.

What were the chances that I'd simply brought him back to life with normal human means?

Slim.

Maybe it was because he wasn't the seventh offspring of the seventh son.

No. That had nothing to do with it. It was Rebekah's blood flowing through his veins that would cause him to come back to life, to have another chance. A sudden thought jarred me. What if Rebekah wasn't his mother? Impossible. She was his mother. She'd admitted it.

"Hey! Earth to Jamie." Rob pulled from my hold.

"It's Rouge," Michael barked from the front seat beside me.

"What're you doing?" Rob took my attention again, his eyes filled with questions.

"I was just checking your color and making sure you were okay. You scared me back there." I shrugged and turned, taking my seat again and letting my analysis of the situation die down. Nothing was going to be solved as quickly as I liked.

Maybe the transition took longer with boys?

I growled and looked over at Michael as he lifted an eyebrow at me.

"What's on your mind, Rouge?" He pulled into a fast food burger restaurant and stopped by the order-board.

"We'll talk later. I'll take a number one, plain and dry." I stared out the window closest to me and ignored the rest of my friends as they placed their orders.

With so much to figure out, I did what I usually did when overwhelmed. Nothing. I shut down, forcing all thoughts from my head.

I needed a warm meal, maybe take a long bath and then snuggle up next to Michael and hope for a good night of sleep. Tomorrow I could spend the day working through the events of the fight and how everything turned out so poorly. I could lament over my mother's death and the horrible way I ended things with her, but not tonight.

Michael handed the food bags to me and drove to the closest hotel.

We all piled out of the SUV and waited outside as Michael went in and got us two rooms. After locking the vehicle, we moved into one of the rooms and huddled around the table, eating fast and furiously, ignoring each other. I realized then that I hadn't had more than a bag of chips and a soda over the last twenty-four hours.

I needed to be more responsible. A new life was growing in me. It wasn't just about me anymore.

"I can't believe what the hell's going on. We were supposed to get in, get Rob, get out." Michael sat back and ran his hands through his blond hair, his eyes focused on me. "All of those hunters... dead."

He didn't say anything else, but I heard *my brother's words* on the tip of his tongue. He knew better than to say the words out loud.

"I want to know how the hell they died. What the hell happened?" Rob took another bite of his third hamburger and leaned farther in toward us. "It was like a dark cloud settled over the place."

"I didn't see a cloud." Grace crossed her arms over her chest. "I saw everyone running around as if insane, but no cloud."

"I didn't see a cloud either," Michael added and reached out to me, squeezing my arm softly. "Did you?"

"I need to figure out what exactly happened. I'm pretty sure it's related to the dark angel I've mentioned a few times, but I need to be sure." I nibbled at a fry as images of the darkness swept in front of me.

"Hey, stay here with us, okay? Your eyes are shifting to black." Michael tightened his hand around my arm. "I don't want you going through any more today."

I nodded and let out a soft sigh. "I'm here, and I'm fine." I stood. "Just need a bathroom break." When I walked into the bathroom I leaned my head against the door and listened to their conversation. The three of them went straight into a deep conversation over the dark angel.

"Right, but we need to be really clear here. We're not just dealing with Bentos now... but some other evil force?"

"It appears so." Grace kept her voice low. "Apparently Rouge can speak to it or something."

"What?" Rob's word rose sharply.

I flushed the toilet, washed my hands and went back out to them.

Rob glanced up at me as I returned. "What do you know about the dark angel?"

"Not much, I'll find out more after a night of sleep. I'm going for a quick walk to get some air and digest my food. I'll be back." I headed to the door.

"Uh-uh." Michael stood.

"Why not?" I snapped. My anger wasn't meant to be directed at him. "I just need some fresh air." I bit my tongue, ready to cry.

"You're not going on your own. I'm coming with you." Michael moved up beside me and opened the door. "You guys want to split the rooms by girls in one and boys in the other?"

"No!" Grace and Rob said at the same time. "You guys take the other and we'll stay in this one."

Michael growled as I tugged him from the room, letting the door close behind us.

"Grace is old enough to be a big girl."

"No, she's not," he mumbled.

"She's the same age as you. And it's my brother."

"That's the point. He's a Grollic."

Despite the pain of the day, I started laughing. "Really? Our mother died today, Caleb wants us dead, Rob did die today. We're probably not going to make the week and it bothers you he's a Grollic? So am I. You don't seem to mind sleeping with your Grollic." I slid my arm around the back of his waist and tucked myself against his side as we walked out into the peaceful evening. "Get over it, Michael."

Chapter 6

"Grace is making a mistake by snuggling up to your brother. We both know it."

Michael's words hit me wrong and I tugged away from him. Had we just discussed this? Or maybe I had. An agitated sigh left Michael and I stopped at the edge of the parking lot and turned to face him. "And why is caring about Rob a mistake? Because he's a Grollic?"

"No!" Michael's brow tightened. "But whether anyone wants to talk about it or not, once Bentos is taken out, his kind dies with him. We all know that. It's going to be hard enough trying to help you grieve your brother's passing, but to have Grace falling apart too?" He huffed. "I can't keep dealing with all this shit!"

"So sorry we're going to inconvenience you." I turned and stomped toward the darkness of the forest up ahead. Anger burned in my belly and I ignored Michael calling to me from behind. He could give me a minute to burn off a little bit of steam before I let hell loose on him. He was being pissy—again.

"Rouge. Stop walking so fast. You know it's true and if you'll just stop and think..."

I spun around and moved toward him so fast he didn't have time to realize I was standing in front of him. He stumbled backward as a fist I didn't know I'd made punched his chest. "I know it's true, but you can't help who you fall in love with. Obviously." I was being a jerk and I knew it, but with all the tension building up around us, mine was soon to explode on someone. Might as well be Michael.

"What's that supposed to mean? If you had a choice, what? You'd be with Joshua?" He crossed his arms over his chest and peered down at me like he had uncovered some great secret.

"What? No. Why would you..." I threw my hands in the air and let out a growl. "Let it out, Michael. All of a sudden something's bothering you and I don't think it's Grace and Rob. Let it out, because things are going to get even more complicated after tonight."

"Fine. It's you who's asking for it." His words were biting and his expression impossibly tight. "Have you slept with anyone besides me?"

His words hit me like a ten-ton pile of bricks. I couldn't even respond for a minute, which seemed to answer the question incorrectly for me.

"I see," he mumbled, his face falling and eyes dimming.

"You see? What? No! Of course I didn't! I've only been with you that one night we shared together." I hugged myself, though the logical thing would have been to comfort him. Except I'd been through too much to now have to deal with Michael's insecurities.

He jerked his head up and took a step closer. "You didn't sleep with Joshua?"

"No! Of course not. I had just told you that I loved you. Why would I share myself with someone I didn't love?" I shook my head, trying hard not to let the disgust over his question change my desire to snuggle up to him for the night. I was beyond tired and after all we'd once again been through, I wanted to feel loved and safe, not attacked for being a whore of sorts.

"So the baby is mine?" He lifted an eyebrow, obviously not having heard me.

I reached out to slap him hard across his cheek as anger burned the inside of my chest. I went to slap him again, the heat on my hand offering a minute amount of satisfaction.

He caught my hand and pulled me close, wrapping me in a tight hug and pinning my arms by my side. Soft kisses covered my chin and cheeks before a longer one rested on my lips.

I wanted to be angry, to jerk away, but the comfort of being in his arms melted me. I lifted to my toes and pressed against his mouth, giving into the warmth he offered.

Once he released my arms, I slid them around his neck and held him tightly to me, extending the kiss and taking my time to reassure him that I only belonged to him. I couldn't even fathom kissing another man, much less sleeping with one.

"I'm sorry," he whispered as he pressed his forehead to mine. "Forgive me. I just couldn't get past the fact that Joshua was supposed to be your mate. I figured that meant..."

He couldn't seem to say it, and I didn't want him to anyway.

"Well, it didn't." I brushed another soft kiss by his lips.

He let out a shaky sigh and moved back, taking my hand into his and walking us farther into the forest. "I feel so much better."

"Good. The baby's yours, I'm yours and we have one hell of a fight ahead of us." I glanced over at him and tugged on his hand. "I'm not killing Bentos until I understand how to save Rob."

"This can't be about one person." He stopped and pinned me with a staunch look.

"And if it were Grace's life? You would sacrifice it?" I forced myself to keep holding his hand though everything inside of me screamed to pull from him once again.

"Point taken." He ran his free hand through his hair and let out a frustrated groan. "Why does this have to be so damn complicated?"

"Because everything is." I moved to a stone bench that rested under a large oak tree and sat down. The moon sat high in the sky, illuminating the area around us where there was a break in the cluster of branches from the trees. "Come sit down and rest for a minute with me."

"I'm so tired of nothing working out. I keep thinking eventually we'll get a break or something will tilt in our favor, but it just hasn't." He sat down next to me and wrapped a strong arm around my shoulders. "Nothing in my life has worked like it should and I just keep waiting for something to happen to us. I know it's stupid, but fear won't allow me to just rest in the fact that we're forever. The night Bentos took your life in the forest..."

He paused and I nestled against him, tucking my face into his neck and trying to keep my own emotions at bay. Michael rarely opened up. This was a golden opportunity to see him raw and unprotected. I wanted it. Needed it.

"I thought I was going to die too," he whispered and kissed the side of my face.

"But I didn't die and neither did you. We're going to get through this together and when we do, we're going to find an island far from everyone and just spend a few years raising our child and loving on each other. Deal?" I glanced up and smiled.

"I'd like that a lot." He smiled tightly. "Do you think it's a boy or a girl?"

His fingers brushed over my stomach a few times before stopping and cupping the small swell where the child lay.

"I don't know, but I need to get to a doctor soon to have a checkup." I glanced up at the sound of an owl calling out above us. My eyes were capable of locating the animal and focusing on the curve of its small feathers, though it was far too dark around us for that to make sense.

"I'm not sure your hunter status would allow for that. You don't have a human physiology anymore. It would probably cause more problems than we know what to do with." He kissed my shoulder and rested his cheek against me. "This is new water we're treading on." He sighed and rubbed his eye with his free hand. "I'm so tired."

"Me too." I brushed my fingers through his hair and let out a long breath. It felt good to sit in the silence with the one person I knew would always be beside me. We'd had a rough start and it just seems to continue to get harder and harder to remain together, but we were doing it. The end was in sight. I just needed to figure out how to take out my father while protecting my brother and saving my baby. *Not complicated at all. Ha!*

"It's cold out here. Let's get you inside and try to have a good night's sleep. Something tells me it's going to be a rare occasion from here on out." Michael stood and extended his hand to me.

I took it and bit at my lip for a minute, trying to think through all that had happened. If I were able to project the darkness onto certain people in a crowd, then maybe I could attack Bentos, but not anyone else. That was possible, but attacking him wasn't the issue. Killing him was.

"What're you thinking about?" Michael squeezed my fingers.

"I have to find a way to save my brother, and not only him, but the other Grollics who are truly innocent. Bentos uses them for evil, but I figure almost eighty percent of them are just trying to live the life they've been given." I expected a fight from the handsome hunter beside me, but didn't get one.

"Look in your journal and see if there is a way to link the Grollics to you." He lifted his hand and coughed. "I don't like the idea of leaving any Grollics alive, but I understand your point. Your brother isn't evil, a huge pain in the ass, but not evil."

I popped his chest playfully as we reached the door to their hotel room. "Do we dare go in?"

"You do it. If I see something I shouldn't, I'm liable to tear the room apart in order to get my hands around his throat." Michael backed up and lifted his hands, clasping them behind his head and walking toward the other room he'd rented for the night.

I opened the door, only to slam it shut quickly. Grace was sitting on top of my brother, clothed from what I could tell, but something told me that was soon to change.

"Yep. They're sound asleep. Let's go to our room." I walked quickly toward our room as Michael growled. He knew me far too well to get away with lying.

"I don't want to know anything about it." He moved to the door and worked to get it opened before pushing it open for me. "Not a word."

"I'm not saying anything." I let out a nervous laugh and walked into the chilled hotel room. After kicking off my shoes, I dropped down on the bed and let out a sigh of relief. "Can we just stay here forever?"

"It'd be expensive, and knowing you, you'd get bored, but sure. If it would make you happy." He crawled up to hover on top of me, his body draped across me from the chest up. He seemed to be protecting my tummy by not laying completely on top of me.

"I love you so much," I murmured and lifted my head while pulling him down for a long kiss.

He turned us on our sides and pulled me in tightly before picking up where we left off on our make-out session. The smell of his soap mixed with the lingering hint of his cologne made the world melt around me.

I let go of the worries I had sitting so heavily on me and focused on my future.

"We need to get married before the baby comes. I want that union between us if you'll have me as your husband." He kissed my lips again before moving to my neck.

"Are you asking me to marry you?" I chuckled as he jerked his head up.

"No. I mean, yes. Well... no. I want to do it with a ring and in the right way, but I assumed it was the next step for us." He lifted his eyebrow, obviously knowing how badly he'd butchered the moment.

"A ring sounds good for some time in the near future." I brushed my hand down the side of his face. "I'd marry you for a hot bath right now though."

He smiled and shook his head before crawling off the bed backwards. "I'll run you some water."

"Thank you." I sat up and tugged Michael's Sioghra from under my t-shirt. The dark blood moved around as if it had a life of its own. I ran my thumb over the ornate heart and brought it to my lips, kissing it once and tucking it back into my shirt.

"Come test the temperature," Michael called to me from the bathroom.

"Do you think the baby will be born human, Grollic or already be a hunter?" I moved into the bathroom and pulled my shirt over my head.

Michael stood and moved toward me, his eyes running down the length of my body and giving me chill-bumps. He reached behind me and unclasped my bra while leaning in and kissing softly at the skin just below my ear. More chill-bumps, followed by a shiver.

"I'm not sure I want to know. I guess we'll have to wait and see." He moved back and sat on the toilet, not at all shy about watching me while I finished undressing and got in the tub. "Scoot up and I'll wash your back for you."

I sunk into the hot suds and turned carefully to give him my back. He worked slowly to rub a soft hand-towel over the sore muscles of my shoulders and back while leaning over the top of me. His fingers traced my Grollic birthmark and even though I couldn't see his face, I knew he was studying it intently. It didn't bother me, nor give me the urge to shy away or hide it. He knew it was part of who I was and I wasn't ashamed of it anymore.

"That feels good." I pressed my head to my knees and let out a long exhale, finally starting to relax. We had so many things to discuss, namely how the darkness came out of me and why it had happened back at the facility, but now wasn't the time. I was given a precious opportunity to relax into the capable hands of my boyfriend, my hunter.

"You're so beautiful, Rouge. I'm not sure I tell you that enough." He brushed his hand over my hair and leaned down, kissing me once more. "Enjoy your bath. I'll wait for you in the bed."

I nodded as nervousness rose up inside of me. Did he expect something of me in terms of sex? I wasn't sure, but I let the thought go. He was mine forever and we would work all things out as we came upon them.

I finished up and dried off as my breathing got off kilter. Wrapping the towel around me, I walked out to find Michael in the bed, his waist covered with the sheets, but his chest bare and expression relaxed. He turned from blankly watching the TV and smiled.

"Feel better?"

"Much." I moved to the sink and finished getting ready for bed before picking up my dirty t-shirt.

"Don't put that on. It's just me. Come here and let me hold you and we'll get you something new to wear in the morning." He patted the bed next to him and I nodded, walking over and letting the towel drop before joining him.

The click of the remote had the TV going off and the world around us plunged into darkness. Michael reached for me, pulling me in tightly and wrapping his arms around me.

"I love you so much, baby. I thought I'd lost you again when we were at Caleb's. You trusted me and I failed you. Forgive me?"

I snuggled up against him, enjoying the feeling of his body against mine more than I remembered doing last time. "You were betrayed, Michael. There's nothing to forgive." I pulled him down and captured his lips, not willing to talk about all we'd done right and wrong over the last few years. I was tired and wanted the moment to be about us. Nothing else.

Chapter 7

Michael wasn't in the room the next morning, when I woke. However, I didn't panic... well, I didn't panic until after I put my ear to the wall of the room beside us and made sure there were no bodies slamming against the walls or fighting going on. Michael gone, probably to get breakfast, gave me time to take a long shower and start to process some of what happened the day before. The journal had to hold the key to why the Grollics were linked to my father's life force and whether or not there was a way to break it or shift it.

If I could free my people in the process of taking out the greatest evil known to earth, I'd win on both ends. My brother would be free and all those who were alive and still hell-bent on bringing havoc and unrest would be hunted down by the hunters and destroyed. Their job wouldn't be over with the destruction of Bentos, but would be a lot easier.

I pulled out the journal from the backpack left perched on the chair beside the bed and sat down at the tiny round table near the door, tucking my feet under me and wishing I had something besides a dirty t-shirt to put on.

I found the pages in the center of the journal about my father and his creation being a gift from the dark spirit. To see that demon mentioned in the old book sent tendrils of fear down my spine. He'd been there the whole time, but the pages were just now opening up to me, which could mean only one thing. The end was coming soon.

"Why are the Grollics tied to Bentos and not M...?" I stopped myself from saying his name. It would only take the whisper of his ancient name and he would appear. I needed a long incantation to bring my father to me, or I could simply put great power on display and he would arrive to witness it and outdo me, as he had several times now.

I needed to know if there was a way to tie the Grollics to me. I didn't at all want the responsibility, but at least in having it, I could kill Bentos and not have a thousand unplanned deaths on my hands. Only one. Only his.

The door opened and Michael stuck his head in. His blond hair was disheveled and his eyes filled with kindness.

"Hey. You're up." He moved into the room and took the seat opposite of me, his eyes moving to the journal and then back up to me.

"Yeah. I took a quick shower. I need some new clothes." I shut the journal and tugged at the large t-shirt I wore. "This was from the cabin we stopped at a day or so ago."

"I'm aware." He nodded to the floor by the bed. "I went into town earlier and got you some jeans and a new t-shirt. There are some socks in there too."

I turned and smiled. "Awesome. I didn't see the bag earlier."

"Meet me in the other room after you've dressed. Rob and Grace are up and have some donuts and juice for us." He moved to the door before pausing. "You feeling okay?"

My cheeks colored as I nodded and adverted my eyes. We'd made love the night before and Michael was terrified that he was going to hurt the baby. I had reassured him ten times that everything was fine, but concern still sat on him.

He crossed the room and pulled me into his arms, leaning down to brush a kiss by my lips. "Good. Get ready and let's get on with this. Our island is calling."

I chuckled and pulled from him, waiting until the door closed to strip out of my t-shirt and change into the outfit he picked up for me. It fit perfectly, but I wasn't surprised at all. His attention to detail was impeccable.

After gathering the journal and my backpack, I moved out into the midmorning air. A few cars passed on the large freeway in front of the hotel, but other than them, the morning was silent. Serenity rested on my shoulders and for the first time in a long time, I felt a sense of peace.

It wouldn't last, but I needed to remember the feeling so I wouldn't forget what we were fighting for.

Michael knew that I was pregnant, and that the baby was his. My focus was sharpening where my skills were concerned and the new player in the game was stacking up to be more of a friend than a foe. I'd never tell Michael, Grace or Rob that, but the dark spirit had assisted me far more than attacked.

The fact that he was Michael and Grace's father had to have something to do with it. I pressed the door open to catch Rob in mid-sentence.

"... yeah, but is evil really capable of love?"

I dropped my bag by the door as Grace stood and offered her seat. "Sit down and eat."

I took the seat, which was next to Rob, who sat on the bed, and plucked the chocolate donut from his fingers, the thing untouched and looking divine.

"We're talking about the dark spirit from Michael's dreams." Rob glanced back at me and eyed the donut. "Eat it fast or it's mine again."

Grace handed him another donut and turned her gaze on me. "Michael said it wasn't just his dream, but yours too. Is that the only time you've seen this thing?"

"No." I finished my bite of donut, savoring the freshness and sweetness in my mouth before continuing, "I saw it—him— several times in Colorado. I was just thinking about it in the other room." I took another quick bite of the donut and tried to talk around it. "I'm not sure he's capable of love, but to use us for his own purposes? Yes. He would do that. I believe that without a shadow of a doubt."

"Was that who you called to defend you in the forest when we were fighting Bentos?" Michael took the seat closest me and leaned over, pressing his forearms to his thighs.

"Yes. I didn't know what else to do. Something happened between my father and the dark angel a long time ago. I'm not sure what, but they aren't at all on the same side anymore." I turned my attention back to my breakfast as my stomach growled loudly.

"Has to be a boy." Rob reached back and rubbed my tummy. "He's going to be big and strong like his Uncle Rob. Feed him the whole damn dozen."

Michael rolled his eyes and reached out, squeezing my knee softly. "Do you have information on the dark angel?"

"The journal has some information in it, but honestly I think our best bet is to go back to Colorado to my father's house. There's a hidden room in the bottom of the house that I'm sure is a treasure trove of sorts."

"How do you know that?" Rob glanced back.

"Joshua mentioned it one of the times we were talking about things. He didn't necessarily say there would be information or books there, but he said it had a lot of Bentos' belongings down there."

"Caleb would know the answers too." Michael sat back and crossed his arms over his chest. "I wish we could trust him."

"But we can't," Rob threw in his thoughts quickly.

"So what is the plan, gang? We can't sit here talking about everything while the world goes on dissolving around us. We have to strike Caleb out of the picture." Grace stood and started to move around the room, gathering things and throwing them into a dirty laundry bag. "I think we should head back to Bentos' cabin and see what we can find."

"You don't think he's there, do you?" Rob moved to get another donut, handing one to me and taking two for himself.

"I don't know, but he's not ready to fight."

"How can you be sure of that?" Michael pinned me with a hard stare.

"He told me yesterday at the facility when he unleashed darkness on all of the hunters around us." I shrugged and bit into the sugary goodness between my fingers.

"And was that him who unleashed that same evil in the warehouse when Grace and I were fighting and you were getting Rob?" Michael's question was probing and I didn't want to answer it, but I knew I had to.

"No," I whispered and glanced down, not quite sure I was ready to talk about it.

"Was it you?" Rob asked, taking his place beside me on the bed again. He reached out and squeezed my shoulder. "It's okay if it was, Jamie."

"Rouge," Michael barked.

I nodded and focused on my brother. "It was me, and try to remember to call me Rouge, okay? I don't know this Jamie girl and can't remember ever being her."

Rob nodded and squeezed my shoulders, though a hint of hurt brushed across his face. "Sure. Of course."

"How did you unleash the darkness that came from your hands, Rouge?" Michael moved into Rob's spot as my brother got up and started packing up the remaining donuts.

"I just felt it bubble up inside of me and I let it out. I did the same thing in Caleb's backyard." I finished my breakfast and licked my fingers. "I don't think it's a new power that's been opened up for me. I think it was a buildup of darkness from the dark spirit."

"A buildup of darkness? What do you mean?" Grace paused by the door with a small bag against her chest and her arms hugging it tightly.

"Bentos told me yesterday that the dark angel has a price. I assume that means if you call on him for aid that you harbor some of his darkness. It comes tumbling out of you without warning, which is what happened in the warehouse yesterday." I stood and shook my head. "Let's talk about this more later. The idea of harboring anything evil gives me the creeps."

"Me too." Rob shivered and opened the door, holding it open wide for everyone. "So we're heading back to Colorado?"

"Yes. I think that's our best bet. You?" I glanced toward Michael to see if he felt differently.

"It appears that that's our best course of action. Let's start that way and if something else comes up, we'll deal with it then." He touched my lower back and walked beside me to the SUV.

"I want to talk a little bit about what we plan on doing with the fact that Bentos' life is tied to all Grollics. Does that mean that when we kill him, I die too?" Rob extended his hand toward Michael. "Keys. I'll take the first leg of the trip."

I was surprised to see Michael hand over the keys without a fuss. It seemed a few weeks back that any reason to argue with my brother was a good one. Maybe things were changing.

"I don't like that ending at all." Grace got in the front seat as Michael and I piled in the back.

I buckled up and reached between my legs to get my journal out of my backpack. "I was looking into that earlier. I think the weirdest part is that if the dark angel was the creator of the Grollics, then why isn't he the one that's tied to them?"

"Because somewhere along the way, things were shifted to rest on the seventh son of the seventh son, "Michael said."

I flipped through the pages of the old book as Rob pulled us back onto the highway, headed west.

"But you're the seventh," Rob spoke from the front seat.

"So you think if Bentos dies, that the connection will shift to my shoulders?" I asked.

"I would think so, but it would be a horrible tragedy if we were wrong." Rob shrugged and I held my agreement, everyone in the vehicle already knowing my thoughts on the subject.

"I honestly think there has to be a way to shift the burden back to the dark spirit. If he had the connection, then killing Bentos wouldn't cause the destruction of the Grollics." Grace turned and faced me and Michael.

"I think that's the answer, but the only problem is that we need to take out the dark spirit too." I glanced up. "He's pure evil. Any help he's provided me has been for his own purposes. Of that I'm sure."

"Why do we keep calling him a dark spirit?" Rob adjusted the rearview mirror to see me.

"Because if you call out his name, he appears." I turned my attention back to the book.

"This is too much to work through the way we're doing it," Michael growled softly and leaned back in his seat. "I think first thing is first. We figure out the power of three and what it's going to take to kill Bentos."

"Yeah, but that's useless information if we aren't going to kill him." Grace turned back around in her seat.

"We are going to kill him," Michael responded.

"Not until we disconnect the Grollics' life source from him." I fingered through the pages, listening and not really paying attention. "The power of three... the chosen three... what is it?" I murmured, not sure if I'd said the words out loud. I stared blankly through the window trying to think through what could create the power of three, not because I was ready to harness such a weapon, but because I couldn't help myself.

Rob's amber gaze caught my attention and I locked onto him in the small mirror. If he'd died yesterday, why weren't his eyes blue?

"Are you sure Rebekah was your mother?" I asked, unable to help myself.

He stared at me oddly and then slowly nodded. "As sure as I can be, I guess. Why?"

"No reason, just trying to think through the drama of what happened yesterday." I looked back to the journal, grateful that no one peppered me with questions.

"What about the power of three? We're going to need it soon. We need to get any remaining items that are needed." Michael slid his hand over the top of my thigh and rested it there as he turned his face toward me.

"We originally thought it was the journal, me and the Sioghra, but that proved false." I closed the book and turned my attention to my handsome boyfriend. "Rob and I thought it might be three people just because the old prophecy says that the power of three will stand against the enemy. People stand."

"That's true." Michael rubbed his fingers over his mouth and looked off into the distance. "Do you think it's me, you and Grace? You, Rob and Grace? Me, Grace and Rob?"

"I think Rouge is definitely part of it," Rob threw in his two cents.

"Me too." Grace turned and smiled at me. "I'm not sure it could be one of us without the other though."

"What? What do you mean?" Michael questioned her.

"We're twins, so if it's Rouge and two other people, and one of them is Rob... it wouldn't be one of us. Where you go, I go sort of thing."

He nodded and sucked his bottom lip into his mouth. "It would be the two of us and Rouge, but something tells me that Rob is a part of it too just because of the way things have played out."

"Maybe it's just me." I offered up and sunk back into my seat.

"But you're not three people." Michael smiled, lifting his eyebrow. "Right? Something you're not telling us?"

"I'm a Grollic. I'm a hunter." I paused, searching my head for another answer. "I'm..."

"Beautiful." He moved over and pulled me in tightly.

"Aw, Damn. Not this." Rob laughed as Grace swatted at him.

The conversation would no doubt come up again, but with missing pieces of the puzzle, we were running in the same old circles. Hopefully the basement at Bentos' log cabin had a few more clues to solving the riddle.

If not, Caleb might be our only hope. Scary thought.

Chapter 8

We stopped for a meal four hours later namely due to the fact that I was turning into a total bitch because of hunger.

Rob pulled off the road and parked near the back of the restaurant because it was so busy, which seemed odd for a weekday night, but perhaps not.

"I'm going to rearrange the stuff in the back. I want to know if there are any weapons from the previous owners."

Grace laughed. "It has nothing to do with the extra pillow *someone* stole from the hotel?"

"You stole that pillow!" Rob pretended to be shocked.

Grace popped him in the chest and laughed.

"Oh, right." He got out and I followed him to the back after urging Grace and Michael to go in and get us a table.

"You doing okay? You've been driving for a long while." I reached out and rubbed my hand along the top of my brother's back.

"Yeah, just a lot to think about." He took a shaky breath, glanced around and turned to me. "What happened at the facility? I don't remember much of it. It's all kind of a blur."

"You tell me what happened when we got to Caleb's and I'll fill in the end of the story." I sat down on the edge of the open trunk and patted the spot beside me.

"Right," Rob stared and turned, sitting down beside me. "I went with Grace to the backyard in search of Sarah and Caleb while you and Michael went into the study that day. It wasn't but a few minutes after stepping out in the backyard that a large guy grabbed me and wrestled me to the side of the house. Mother came out of nowhere, poked me in the neck with a needle and I was out."

Anger burned through me. "She drugged you?"

"Yes, but it was for my own good. If I'd have changed in front of them, all of them would have attacked me." He ran his hand through his mop of curly brown hair. "I was so hurt at first, thinking that she had turned against me, but she told me that she was on my side when we reached the facility."

"I figured out how to access your location with the journal, if you're wondering," I interjected into the story, knowing he was going to ask about it if I didn't.

"I figured you'd mastered some new trick. Pretty handy if you ask me." He snorted. "I could see you the one time you came into the back of the van with me."

"I came twice, but the first time you were out cold." I clasped my hands together and squeezed tightly. "I was so mad at Rebekah. I was sure she was involved and had turned against us."

"No. Never. Not for a million dollars." He reached up and pressed his fingers against his eyes. "She died trying to save us in that warehouse, didn't she?"

"You don't remember?" I glanced over toward him.

"It's really fuzzy. I think I was drugged again at the facility, because I can get bits and pieces of what happened, but no real picture."

I reached over and wrapped an arm around his upper back, pressing my head against his shoulder and relaxing. "I'm not going to let anything happen to you."

He laughed. "That's my line, silly girl."

"I know, but I want you to know that I'll not raise a hand to Bentos until I know you're safe from the effects of killing him."

"And I want you to know that when the time comes, you need to do whatever you need to do to bring his life to an end, Rouge.

If that means the Grollics die in the process, then so be it. I'm willing to sacrifice myself for the greater good."

"There is no good in wiping out a race of people." I jerked back as emotions overwhelmed me.

"Yes, there is." He smiled and stood. "Tell me one more thing and then let's get in there before your baby daddy loses his shit."

I smirked and forced the burn of tears back. I didn't care what my brother was willing to sacrifice. I was being selfish and wasn't willing to lose him. Period.

"What do you want to know?" I helped to reposition the stolen pillows and we closed the door.

"Why did you ask if Rebekah was my mother? You have something running through that complicated mind of yours. I just know it." He reached out and ruffled the top of my head.

I swatted him away and brushed my hair back down as we walked toward the restaurant.

"Because, when I died in the forest with Bentos and Michael, I came back alive as a hunter." I turned to him and let my eyes bleed blue.

"What the hell?" He jumped back and let out a soft yelp.

"Right. No one but Michael and Seth know, well, and Bentos I would imagine." I let out a long exhale and paused in front of the doors to the restaurant. "I expected the same to happen to you yesterday."

"What? Why? I didn't die." He crossed his arms over his chest as if to protect himself from the truth that raced through him.

"Yes. You did." I shook my head as the scene rushed past my gaze. I had been calm and rather collected, but inside of me I was frantic, terrified and lost to the idea of letting my brother die.

"You're sure of it?" He reached out and touched my arm as tears filled my eyes.

I glanced up at him as the first one rolled onto my cheek. "Yes. No breath, no heartbeat and the light in your eyes was gone."

"Oh, Jamie. Don't cry." He pulled me close and wrapped me in a big bear hug.

I let myself feel the sadness and fear that there might not be too many of those hugs left if I didn't figure this thing out with my father soon.

"I'm not going anywhere." He squeezed me one more time and moved back a little. "We'll figure this out, okay?"

"I know. I'm just scared that it won't be in time. I'm tired of fighting and giving everything to lose each time." I shrugged and wiped my tears away angrily.

Rob blinked in rapid succession and got in my face with a goofy grin on his face. "My eyes blue now?"

"No. Silly."

He blinked slowly, far more exaggerated. "Now?"

"No. Idiot." I swatted at him and opened the door as Grace pressed her face to it with a look of impatience. "I'm telling you that something about what happened with you yesterday isn't right."

"I wasn't dead. Simple really," he mumbled at my back as we walked into the warmth of the large cafe.

I turned and pinned him with a hard stare. "Yes. You were."

We ate our fill of fried southern food and forced ourselves back to the SUV as the sun was setting in the sky.

"Who's up for driving? I have to take a nap and let my food-baby digest." Rob puffed his stomach out and rubbed it slowly.

"I'll drive." Michael took the keys and turned to me. "You need to take a nap too. You have to take care of yourself."

I chuckled, unwilling to respond with a snarky remark like I usually would. He was playing the protective father for the baby inside my stomach and not so much for me.

I nodded and turned to Grace. "You okay up front with Michael?"

"Yes. I need to discuss with him about that crap Caleb said the other day." She opened the door and winked at me. "Besides, I like giving him hell anyways."

I smirked and got in the SUV, taking Rob's offered hand for assistance and snuggling down with one of the stolen pillows. Guilt swelled up inside of me over not telling Michael and Grace what I knew about the dark angel being their father, but it was a conversation that was far more suited when we had time to dissect the implications and after I gained more proof. Starting them on a search for the truth with a possible lie wasn't the right way to go about things.

It didn't take more than a few minutes and I was lost to the waking world.

Dark trees loomed around me, swaying softly back and forth as the moonlight hid from us. I turned in a quick circle, taking note that Rob and Michael were at my back and Grace by my side. We were surrounded by Grollics under the control of evil.

Their teeth were bared and spittle dripped from angry jowls as their warnings filled up the night around us.

Bentos moved out from the darkest parts of the forest and lifted his hand, forcing the three Grollics closest to him to stand on their hind legs.

"I'm glad you've figured out the secret to your success, daughter." His voice was filled with pride.

"You'll die tonight because of it," I responded coolly. I knew how to kill him and I'd pulled the tie between him and the Grollics off of his shoulders. I could slaughter him and never harm one of them.

"I will. You're right, but so will one of your beloved." He winked and rushed at Grace, picking her up and throwing her toward a

large tree. She hit it with a sickening crack and the Grollics attacked.

I couldn't get to her because of the onslaught of beasts rushing toward me, readying for the fight of their lives.

"Don't let them bite you," Michael cried out.

I worked to get through them, twisting and turning as I threw their large bodies and cracked a few of their necks. It wasn't a time to feel burdened by offering death. They were harbingers of pure evil in that moment.

Bentos circled Grace as he laughed deeply from his chest.

I pushed forward, but realized I'd never make it in time. I spun, throwing a solid punch into a large brown wolf's muzzle. My eyes scanned the scene behind me. Rob and Michael were fighting furiously, Rob having transformed into a large amber wolf. They would be no help in rescuing Grace.

There was a cost to call on the help that I needed, but I wasn't willing to watch my best friend die because of my own failures.

I turned in time to see Bentos lift a long blade into the air.

"Malaz," I screamed. "Aid me and I will repay your costs."

Bentos turned and growled loudly as a dark shadow picked him up and twisted him around in the air above us.

I raced toward Grace, pulling her up and getting in her face. "Are you okay?"

"Yes. Thanks for the help." She pushed at me and chuckled. "Let's get back to doing what we do best."

I smiled and picked up my father's blade before lifting my eyes to the heavens. The dark angel shifted from the trees and headed with expedience to the spot just before me. He drove my father into the ground, causing the earth to buckle and shake violently.

I righted myself and moved without a thought in mind, jamming the sword deep into Bentos' chest and screaming out words that came from deep within me. The light in his eyes died and I let out a cry before looking up at the dark-haired angel who watched me with interest.

He was incredibly beautiful, but just beneath the surface of his alabaster skin pulsed dark veins. Evil. I took a step back, realizing that perhaps I was calling on the wrong entity for help.

He nodded toward me and whispered softly, "My cost for my service."

"Is what?" I asked and glanced up, noticing that the fighting had yet to cease. With the Grollics now tied to the dark angel, they beckoned to his call. Why were they still fighting against us? Was that his purpose as well?

He smiled, his teeth black as night. I jerked my face away and only looked up as I heard the agonizing scream of my best friend.

Grace.

The spirit lifted into the sky until I couldn't see him anymore. I was frantic, screaming for him to bring her back, and he did.

He dropped her lifeless body dead. At my feet.

"No!" I screamed and jerked up from my slumber, swinging wildly and trying to break the hold that someone had around me.

"It's me, Rouge. It's your brother. Stop it." Rob squeezed me tighter and I relented, panting softly as I looked around the darkened car.

We were stopped at a convenience store and Michael and Grace weren't in the front.

"Where's Grace?" I pulled from Rob. "Where is she?"

"Hey, calm down. She went in to grab a drink. Come on, let's go in and get you something too. Jeez." He opened the door and offered me a hand. "Bad dream?"

I took in long gulps of air and worked hard at not running toward the store. Fear permeated every cell in my body. The battle couldn't end with my best friend dead at my feet. It had to be a nightmare and not a vision, yet I knew different.

Utilizing the help of Malaz would only bring death and destruction to my door. Why had I thought it would be different? He had to be destroyed. First.

We approached the store and I paused as Michael's voice caught my attention. He was on the phone from what I could tell, and he was agitated.

"I'll be in there in a minute. Just going to check on him." I nodded toward Michael and forced a smile for my brother. "Just a bad dream. I promise. Scared the hell out of me, okay?"

"All right. You want a coke?"

"Yes, Sprite and some chips. Any kind." I turned and walked around the side of the store to see my boyfriend pacing back and forth.

He glanced up and pressed his finger to his mouth as if to tell me to be quiet. I nodded curtly and leaned against the building.

"You lied to me. There is no way around it." Michael let out an exaggerated sigh. "I realize that, but you promised sanctuary. I don't trust you and it's not just me and Rouge now, Caleb. She's pregnant with my child. I don't care what you think about the situation. It is what it is and I'll kill every damn one of you if you try and hurt her or my son. Tell me that you hear me."

I stiffened, not quite sure what to think. Caleb had obviously reached out to Michael. There was no way things would have happened in any other manner.

"I'm not coming home. Neither is Grace. You drew a line in the sand. Period. I've now stepped across it." Michael growled and ran his hand through his hair. "I know I'm like a son to you, but what you've done... it's unforgivable."

I crossed my arms over my chest, feeling the pain of Michael's plait all too well.

"Rebekah died at the facility, Caleb. The fact that she would turn on her own son and daughter leaves me with very little sadness toward losing her." Michael turned to pin me with a stare before walking over and sliding his hand over my neck and cupping it tightly as he watched me.

"She was nothing to me."

He must have meant Rebekah.

"Of course Grace and I want to know more about your reference to us being impure, but not at the cost of returning to you." Michael growled. "Stop beating around the bush. If you want to tell me something... tell me."

Michael pursed his lips and pulled the phone from his ear, dropping the call and letting out a growl. "He wants to see me. He feels the need to explain how I'm intimately connected to not only the dark spirit that you've been playing with, but Rebekah too."

"Rebekah? My mother?"

"Yes." He shook his head and pulled me close. "I don't know what he's getting at, but it's nothing to worry about."

I jerked back.

"Did he say Rebekah was your mother?" Sickness rolled through me at the thought and I shook my head. "That's not possible."

"I agree. It's his hook in my back to get me rushing back home. I don't need to know the truth Rouge. I've lived this long without it. I'll be fine." He pulled me close again, kissing the top of my head.

He would be fine? What if I wasn't? A new fear began forming in the pit of my stomach.

Chapter 9

I got in the front seat of the car as Michael took his place in the driver's seat. I glanced over at him, not quite sure what to say, but wanting to say something. We needed to talk about the possibility of Rebekah being his mother. That would make us...

I couldn't even think it. It wasn't possible. Period.

He turned in his seat and gave me a knowing look. "Stop thinking about it. She's not my mother. He's trying to pull me back in with anything he can find."

"Who was your mother?" I crossed my arms over my chest.

"She was a human female, just like I was at one time. My father was a hunter." He shrugged as if the conversation were going to die there.

"No. Your father is the dark spirit I've been mentioning. That's what Caleb was referring to." I turned to face him, ready for a fight.

"I don't believe that." He shrugged and started the SUV as we waited for Rob and Grace to rejoin us.

"I don't want to believe it, but I'm pretty sure it's true. I want to check the information against anything we can find at Bentos' place. If not..." I hated to say it. "Caleb might be our only true source of information."

"And you want to rely on him?" Michael scoffed. "He just implicated that we're siblings, Rouge. I'm pretty sure he's not willing to be honest with us."

"It's understandable that he's planting a seed of doubt in you." I lifted my hands. "I'm not at all, in any way taking up for him.

I'm just telling you that he's using any weapon at his disposal to bring you back because he loves you."

"Does he?" Michael tapped the wheel and shook his head. "I'm not having anything to do with him for a while. He lied to me and put you and the baby in danger. What would have happened if you hadn't broken free from him? He would have murdered you right in front of my eyes."

"I know," I mumbled and glanced down at my hands. "I just don't know where else we're going to get information from."

"Better hope your father has an archive like we're hoping he does." Michael turned and pursed his lips for a moment before speaking again. "No discussing this in front of Grace. I don't want her worried over nothing."

"Okay," I agreed and leaned back in my seat. "I had a dream when I was in the backseat."

Rob and Grace got in laughing loudly.

I paused until they were settled and talking quietly together to continue.

Michael pulled the car out onto the road and glanced over at me, nodding as encouragement to keep going.

"I'm pretty sure the end result of it is that you, Rob and me are the power of three." I reached up and turned the air vent on me before adjusting it higher.

"Why not Grace?" Michael asked.

"Yeah... why not me?" Grace stuck her head in between our seats. "Wait... why not me what?"

I looked at her and smiled, unable to help myself. "I don't think you're part of the power of three. I think it's me and the two boys."

"I'd say that's no fun, but honestly, it's a huge relief." Grace chuckled again and sat back.

"What makes you think that?" Rob's voice rose up from the back.

"I had a nightmare and it was the three of us, you, me and Michael who fought the Grollics to the end." I shrugged, praying like hell that they didn't ask me where Grace was.

"And where was I? Sipping a fruity beverage on the beach?" Grace laughed again.

Michael glanced over at me, his expression tight. "It's just a dream. Don't make anything of it."

"Right." I wrapped my arms around myself, chilled to the bone all of a sudden.

"Rouge. Where was I?" Grace leaned back up between our seats.

I looked over at her and whispered my response, effectively killing all of the joy in the car. "Dead."

"This place is really hard to find. Help me look for the blue mailbox that was at the edge of the road the last time." Rob looked over at me as we sat in the front seat together. We'd been on the road for far too many hours and both Michael and Grace were passed out in the backseat.

I should have spent the time with Rob trying to figure a few things out, but I was too tired to press into any of it.

"A blue mailbox? I don't remember seeing one the last time we were here." I sat up in my seat and cracked the window a little. Icy cold air blew into the vehicle and Rob shivered, giving me a look.

"It's freezing out there. Roll that up."

I smirked and rolled it up. "You're a werewolf. There is no way you're cold."

"Just because I'm hot blooded doesn't mean I don't get cold. You're hurting my feeling."

"Feeling?"

"Yes. The one that I have." He winked and I laughed.

"Blue mailbox," I yelled and pointed as he started to go past it. A long trail led up into the woods and I recognized the place almost immediately.

"Perfect. Good job." He slowed down, jerking the SUV enough that Michael and Grace woke up.

"This it?" Michael rubbed his face and reached up, squeezing my shoulder softly.

"Yes. There is a lake between us and the house, but there should be a few boats tied up down the ways that we can use." I unbuckled and leaned forward, stretching as my back cracked in several places.

"This place is beautiful." Grace opened her door as Rob pulled the SUV to a stop. "It's peaceful and full of serenity."

"Really? Doesn't Bentos live here?" Michael opened his door and moved to mine, opening it and reaching for me as I got out of the vehicle.

He pulled me into a tight hug before leaning down and kissing me several times.

"What was that for?" I asked, lifting my eyes to rest on his handsome face.

"I just love you. I don't know what's in front of us, but I figure we'll work through it together. Right?" His expression softened and I could see the concern he had over the coming events.

"Right. Absolutely." I moved away from the SUV and took his hand before walking to find Rob and Grace. "My father haunts this place from time to time, but Joshua and his pack lived here."

"Where is his pack now?" Grace stood from helping Rob untie the boat and looked at me.

"No clue. I would assume they scattered, but keep your eyes open for sure. They aren't too sweet on the idea of hunters being on their lands." I got in the small canoe and moved to the far end, sitting down and motioning for Grace to join me.

"You guys go ahead. I'll wait here and Rob can come back for me." Michael leaned over and pushed hard after Rob got in and settled on the opposite end from me.

"There was room, silly." I shook my head, but decided to let it go. We were already moving across the beautiful lake. I didn't want to miss out on the view and the calm that the beauty around me provided.

Leaning over, I skimmed my hand across the water only to jerk it back quickly. A darkness moved just under us and I didn't want to scare anyone, but it shot fear down my spine.

"Something wrong, Sis? Bad memories?" Rob smiled and scooted to his left, which gave me a full view of him.

"Yeah, I guess." I sat statue still in the middle of my seat, not wanting to chance tipping the boat over. Something was below us, and even if it were nothing more than a large fish, I wasn't going overboard again.

We made it to the other side, and I listened carefully to Rob's instructions on how to tie the boat up. After getting it done, I got out and helped Grace and then untied it for Rob to go back across to get Michael.

"Rouge..." Michael called to me, his hands cupped over his mouth, though it wasn't necessary.

"Yeah?"

"Go check in the house to see if we need to get groceries."

Rob threw in his two cents. "I bet there aren't any. I saw a little shopping mall on the way in. Michael and I will go grab some stuff to keep us fed for the next few days."

"We'll go check." Grace smiled and slid her arm into mine. "Let's hope this place is bone dry."

"Why is that?" A smile lifted my lips.

"So that they will be gone for a while and we can have some girl time." She wagged her eyebrows.

I laughed. "Does girl time include you helping me search through the creepy dark basement for more information on the dark spirit?"

She gave me a silly expression. "Well, duh. I wouldn't miss another adventure for anything."

"Right..." I pulled from her and lifted to my toes as we reached the back door. My fingers brushed over the key and I pulled it down, cleaned it off and opened the door for us. We walked in and Grace groaned.

"Yuck. Smells like mothballs in here."

"Go open windows and I'll check the kitchen." I reached for a light, grateful to find that they still worked.

The pantry and refrigerator were completely bare, not a scrap of food anywhere. The dishes were still in place and the living room looked like it hadn't been touched, but whoever took the food planned on not coming back.

I walked back out into the mid-afternoon sunshine and cupped my hands over my mouth. "There's no food. Be careful and hurry back."

"We will," Rob responded.

"No going in the basement alone. Okay?" Michael moved to the edge of the water and I swear my heart melted.

He had to have been the most beautiful man I'd ever seen. Why he wanted anything to do with me was beyond me. I just nodded, knowing that I was headed down there the minute he left.

"You're going down there aren't you?"

"Have I told you how incredibly sexy you are?" I asked, moving toward the water, but stopping short as something moved just under the water's edge.

"Your flattery will get you nowhere." He let out a heavy sigh. "Just be careful?"

"Always." I backed up and moved my attention from him to the water.

"What's the matter? See something?" His voice caught my attention again.

"Yes. No. I don't know." I smiled and turned, jogging back toward the house and away from whatever lurked in the muddy waters of the lake.

"Much better?" Grace finished opening a window and turned to me, waving her hand wildly in the air and coughing. "This place needs to be cleaned something horrible."

"Get it it, Cinderella. I'm not in a cleaning mood." I brushed by her and tugged at her ponytail.

"Michael will do it. He's a clean freak, as if you didn't know."

"I did." I moved down the hall and stopped by the first set of doors as memories rolled over me. Sadness swept through my chest and I reached out, pressing my hand to the door that led down a set of stairs.

The night I'd had the horrible dreams of the dark angel, his claws had sunk deep into my back. The manifestation of that wound came back with me into reality and it was Joshua who took care of me, cleaned me up and held me closely.

Such a good man. What a waste.

"You okay?" Grace touched my shoulder and I jerked. "Hey... it's just me."

"I know. Sorry. Too many memories and I was only here for a few days." I pushed the door open farther as the smell of earthiness rushed up to greet us. "Why does this feel like a bad idea all of a sudden?"

"Because we sit on the precipice of a great adventure?" She gave me a smile, but it didn't manage to reach her eyes. She was a little on edge too. There was no denying it.

"Our adventures never turn out well." I walked down the stairs, pausing only for a moment to reach up in hopes of finding a string that led to a light. I found it and pulled, which illuminated the rest of the stairway, but left the bottom in complete darkness.

"I'm glad you're going first." She stayed behind me, giving me a little bit of space, but not too much. "Why do I keep expecting the door to slam behind us and the light to go out?"

"Because you watch far too many scary movies. That's why." I moved faster, half jogging down the stairs just to get us there. I reached out and flicked the light-switch on the wall and moved around the dank-smelling basement.

Boxes sat upon boxes, the room impossible to think of finding something in.

"Jeez. This is ridiculous," Grace mumbled and moved to a large gun case at the end of the room. "What are we looking for exactly?"

"A safe." I started to push boxes apart in order to see what lay behind them. "If my father has a book on anything as private and as important as the history of the Grollics, then it would be locked away."

"Here's a safe in the floor, or at least I think that's what this is." Grace kicked at something before moving back.

I bent down and used my hands to dust off the stainless steel door. "Great job. That's exactly what this is."

I tugged at it, knowing there was no way it would just open, but trying it once before going to any concerted effort to get into it.

"Locked?" she asked and leaned against a tall stack of boxes.

"Yes, but we'll get into it. I'll try a few codes and if nothing else, we'll have Rob and Michael break into it with some kind of tool or something." I leaned over and started to work through a few combinations that would make sense. I wasn't entirely sure of my birthday, which would have been my first choice.

Grace pilfered around, making various noises as I worked through the last combination that would make sense to me.

"Damn," I grumbled and got up, brushing off my jeans. "We'll have to get the boys to help us when they get back. Come on. Let's get out of here before something crawls out and eats us."

"Not funny." Her face fell and I couldn't help but laugh.

I turned off the light at the bottom of the stairs and glanced up as the door began to close. A large gust of wind blew through the hall from all of the open doors and slammed the door shut.

Grace yelped behind me and I laughed. "Just the wind."

"Yeah, well get us out of here. I hate being underground."

I moved up and opened the door, making room for her to move past me and closing it. We had found the safe, which was good news. If there was anything worth our time it would be in there. If not... Michael might have to call his old mentor. Either way, we were getting a hold of the information we needed to make plans to right the wrongs done to us, and those that came before us.

Chapter 10

"Anyone here?" Rob's voice came through the back window near the kitchen where Grace and I sat at the kitchen table trying to figure out ways that wouldn't get us, Rob in particular, killed.

"Yeah. You guys need help?" I stood and moved to open the back door.

Rob and Michael walked up with their arms full of bags. I reached out and took a few from my brother before urging Grace to do the same.

She let out a spoiled huff, but got up and helped out too.

"Jeez. How long did you think we would be staying here?" I set the bags down and turned to Michael.

"Your brother eats like an animal, and now that you're pregnant, you need to start eating more too." He set his groceries down and shrugged. "Did you girls find anything?"

"A safe." Grace moved up and pulled a banana from the bunch sitting on the counter.

"And? What was in it?" Michael asked.

"We don't know. There's a code and we can't break in." Grace shrugged, obviously annoyed I hadn't told her a way around killing Bentos and all the Grollics without killing Rob. I had no idea how, but I was trying. "There's a large shed out back, maybe you big tough boys can go out there and get some type of tool that'll help you break in."

"I remember that shed." Rob shuddered and snagged Grace's banana, taking a big bite and pressing a sweet kiss to her lips.

"Hey, come on... really?" Michael fussed.

"Yep. Tastes like a banana." Grace took the peel and threw it away.

I popped Michael's butt, trying to warn him to let it rest. They were happy, why couldn't that be enough just for now?

"You and Rob go get the safe open. The light is at the bottom of the stairs and the first door on the left in the hall is the entrance to the basement."

"And what are you going to be doing?" Michael lifted his eyebrow. "Better yet, what is my lazy sister going to do?"

"We'll be cooking," I suggested.

"Cooking? Ugh." Grace winked and walked into the kitchen, starting to work on pulling everything out of bags.

"You cook. She's terrible," Michael whispered before touching the side of my face and leaving.

I barely managed to stifle back a laugh. It wasn't that long ago I remembered how awful Michael was at coffee and cooking—except breakfast, of course. He'd done that one right when we were in the pool house. Our own little place of peace. I sniffed suddenly, my nose feeling the urge to run. Those weren't bad memories. What I had thought was bad back then barely scratched the surface of the horrors of today.

Rob, oblivious to my inner turmoil, followed Michael out, singing something horribly off key.

"Do you think things will ever get back to normal?" I asked, pulling out a large pot from one of the lower cabinets.

"I'm not sure things have ever been truly normal, but I hope we find ourselves living for something else besides 'the fight'. I used to live for this, bored when things grew tedious. Now I find myself tired of running, chasing and fighting. I want to settle down and live a little." She shrugged.

"Once we rid the world of Bentos..."

She cut me off, "And the dark angel."

"Right. Him too." I opened a pack of noodles and ran water in a stainless steel pot. "First we find a way to kill Bentos without destroying all Grollics. Once they're gone, hopefully Caleb and his hunters will turn their attention to any Grollics who still pose a threat."

Grace didn't say anything for a long moment. "I don't know what Caleb will do. All Grollics are evil."

I whipped around only to have her lift her hands in surrender.

"You know I don't believe that, but Caleb, and most hunters, do. Michael and I are part of Caleb's hunters. I'm not sure if we're ever going to be able to change that. Michael's Caleb's understudy. You don't spend decades being an understudy and just let it go in a snap." She shook her head. "You wouldn't get it."

"Being a hunter isn't a choice?" I glanced over my shoulder, not ready to point out that technically I was a hunter now too.

"Not really. It's much like being a Grollic. They have no say in the matter, and we really don't either. We don't know what, or who, we are until after we die. It's not like we get a letter of acceptance in the mail. Think about the old Red Riding Hood story. We were created to hunt. Nothing else." She opened the package of hamburger meat and crumbled it in a pan. "Spaghetti?"

"That's what I was thinking." I pilfered through the bags around me as her words sunk in deep. If she was right, then Michael and I would never truly have a normal life. If we all made it through this, our child didn't stand a chance at having a normal childhood. It would be worse than what I had gone through. Thoughts of my mother and what she gave up to keep me safe made clearer sense. Supposedly she had come back to get me at one point. Maybe it was when Bentos had been out of the picture and when he'd returned she had to let me go again. She'd wanted me, she just couldn't keep me.

"There are so many random snacks in these bags. What were they thinking? We could have cupcakes for dinner and pretzels for breakfast?" She held up various bags of goodies and I laughed.

"Who knows?"

The sound of the back door opening made me glance up. I headed into the living room. I'd forced myself not to think of Joshua here, in this lodge, but it was hard to shake. I swallowed and forced the memories aside. I hadn't loved him, but I'd cared for him and he had died. Bentos had done that. Not me.

Michael and Rob walked in holding two to three tools each.

"Really?" I asked, placing my hands on my hips and trying not to laugh. These strong fighting machines looked silly carrying tools. It was awkward, almost comical

"What? We don't know what will get the damn thing opened." Rob shrugged.

Grace called for help so I headed back into the kitchen and busied myself with getting dinner ready. There was no way I was getting in the middle of the comedy act that was sure to ensue in the basement.

Half an hour later, after loud banging, swearing and yelling, they returned upstairs.

"It's nearly open," Rob said and sniffed. "We need to eat first. I can't think without food."

Table set, food out, we sat down and ate in silence until our bellies were nearly full. Except Rob's.

"This is delicious." Rob held up his fork. A huge wad of spaghetti coated his fork and sauce dripped back onto his plate.

"Good. Grace is a good cook." I took another bite of my dinner and pushed the plate away.

"You only ate half of your food." Michael shook his head. "I— We want a strong boy to raise, Rouge, not some little weakling like your brother."

"Please." Rob lifted his eyebrow and flexed the muscles in his arms and chest.

"Smoking hot." Grace licked at her lips.

"I'm going to be ill." Michael stood and reached for my hand. "Did you say you wanted to check out the safe?"

I laughed and turned to Grace. "Thanks for the help."

"My pleasure." She moved closer to Rob, picking up his fork and feeding him a bite while Michael growled in aggravation.

I pulled him toward the stairs and wrapped an arm around the back of his waist as I chuckled softly. "Leave them alone. There's nothing you can do about it."

"Agreed, but that doesn't mean I have to like it."

"Very true." I opened the basement door and walked down quickly, Rob and Michael having left the light at the bottom on. "Did you see what was in the safe when you got it opened?"

"No. We broke the lock but left the door closed. I figured you'd want to be the first one." He moved in beside me, bending over and lifting the top off of it. The small opening couldn't have been more than a two-by-two space, but a large duffel bag was shoved down into it. "Want me to pull this out?"

"Please?" I moved back as anticipation tore up my insides. "Let's take it upstairs unless it's too heavy."

He grunted and pressed his foot against the side of the safe, twisting back and forth a little to get it out. "Not at all. Let's take it up there. Tell Grace to clear the table."

"Okay." I turned and jogged back up the stairs. "We need the table to open the bag up here."

Grace stood and started to help me clear plates as Rob leaned back and let out a long belch.

"Really?" Grace looked over at him with disgust.

"What? In Germany that means it was an incredible meal." He shrugged.

"No, it doesn't. Now get off your dead ass and help us clean up so we can look through this stuff together." I poked my brother in the side, which assisted in getting him up and busy.

"Fine. Jeez. I gotta do everything around here." He chuckled as everyone turned to give him a look. "Just kidding. Trying to have fun."

Michael came up the stairs and laid the bag on the table when the last dish was cleared. He looked at me. "You open it."

"Okay." I walked up and unzipped it, pulling the sides open and smiling. "Books and journals. Exactly what I wanted."

I handed off three books to each of my friends before taking the oldest three for myself. Rob pulled the empty bag from the table and sat down with us.

"There's something still in here." He bent over and picked up a black velvet bag, pulling out a necklace of sorts, the chain dangling from his fingers. He laid it down and Grace let out a gasp.

"A Sioghra. But whose?" She picked it up and studied it with wide eyes.

"Someone who didn't need it anymore, obviously," Michael muttered, the look in his eyes telling me that he was far more disturbed by Bentos having the item than he was letting on.

I reached out and took it from Grace. "I'll put it in the living room for now and hopefully something in these old books will help us figure out who Bentos was close to."

"We know it wasn't mother," Rob responded, looking up at me.

"True. She had hers until recently." I put the trinket in the small black velvet bag and sat down, pulling one of the old journals toward me as realization rolled over me. "Rebekah didn't have her Sioghra when she died in my arms. Where had it gone?"

"Maybe she gave it to someone," Michael said absently as he licked his fingers and turned the page of the volume that lay before him.

"Then why is there one here? It's empty, which means someone's body created it and the blood is gone, so they're dead now, right?" I know I sounded cross, but I was curious as to how someone's Sioghra survived after their death. The only time I had seen one was when Seth's mate, Tatianna, had died. Seth had crushed it to dust. I couldn't remember if it had been empty or not.

"They were murdered, Rouge. There's an old wives tale that says that if you're murdered and your killer yanks it from your neck before you take your last breath, your soul wanders aimlessly. You don't have the power or the strength to cross over." He looked up briefly, but the sadness in his expression stilled my heart.

"So Bentos murdered a hunter and stole their freedom to ascend?" I couldn't imagine a worst fate.

"Probably." Michael looked back down quickly as Grace closed her book.

"You don't think it was mother, do you?" She turned her question and attention on her brother.

"I once did, a long time ago the thought crossed my mind. After we turned and I went hunting for the truth, I thought mother was one of us, I just... She didn't survive when the Grollics attacked. She was human. Our father was a hunter, not mother... I think." Michael shook his head. "It doesn't really matter anymore. What matters is how we're going to kill Bentos without killing Rob. How are we going to convince Caleb there are Grollics worth saving?" His voice grew louder with his frustration. "What if these freakin' books aren't even in English? Rouge's going to have to read them all?" He slammed his palm on the table. "I want answers! Like who the hell is my father?"

I could see the strain of all we'd been through pressing down on him. "Michael..." I reached out to touch his hand, but he jerked it back.

"No. Don't." He stood and walked to the back door, tugging at his hair and walking out into the sunset.

"I'll go after him." I stood, but took a moment to pull the book he was looking at toward me. The page he was on was ripped clean from the center of the old thing, but the one before showed a shadow rising from the center of a bright light and two humans standing as an extension of the darkness.

Twins... Michael and Grace.

"Michael," I called after him as I walked from the house.

The dull shimmer of his blond hair was all I could make out as he disappeared into the forest. I knew he was frustrated and lost as to what to believe, but I couldn't leave him to suffer that alone.

I jogged toward the forest, pausing only as the brief flutter of angel's wings filled my senses. I turned around slowly and glanced toward the sky, seeing nothing but a million stars.

"Hey," he spoke just behind me and I jumped, yelping loudly.

I spun around and slapped at him before pulling at his t-shirt, forcing him close to me. "You scared me, dick head."

"I'm sorry. I just needed some air." He closed his eyes and breathed in deeply.

I reached up and slid my hands along the side of his face, forcing him to focus on me for a minute.

"I know it's a lot, too much actually, but the truth is worth anything it takes to obtain it or any residual feeling it leaves you with. Ignorance isn't bliss." I leaned in and kissed him softly.

"I agree. I'm just not sure who's telling the truth and who isn't." He pulled from my hold. "And worst of all, this isn't about me right now. We're trying to figure out how to finally take out Bentos. I shouldn't be running around concerned about the past, who my father is. It doesn't matter. What matters is who I am right now."

I'd never heard more poignant words. We were growing up, and it felt like it was happening too fast.

"I agree. Whether your father was the dark angel or not, you're a good man, a strong man and you're going to be a great father."

He glanced down at the ground and kicked a rock toward the forest. "I only have Caleb to thank if I am. He's been a father to me and Grace since we lost our parents. Sarah found us, helped us, but Caleb... he taught me everything. Everything."

I rubbed his back and let him talk without interruption.

"If my father is the dark angel, which is the way it's looking, then Caleb's sacrifice to keep me by his side and call me son had to be that much harder. He must have been waiting all those years to see the darkness bleed through all he had trained me to be."

"But the darkness never did." I slid my arm into his and pressed my head against his shoulder. "If you want to call Caleb and bring him here... then do. But know that I'll kill him before I let him touch me, Rob, or our baby."

"I would kill him before you could get to him if he tries to touch you." Michael turned and pulled me in tightly. "Nothing's going to hurt you again. I won't let it. My loyalty was torn before, but not anymore. Caleb's going to have to understand that I don't stand on the left or the right like I've had to do my whole life. I stand in the middle."

"Me too. Call him." I turned and kissed the swell of Michael's shoulder, more than glad that I came after him.

"I will when the time comes. Let's utilize every other source of information and if we get stuck or need him, I'll call, but it won't be to learn about my past. I'm going to leave that where it belongs."

"Behind us?" I lifted my face toward his, hoping for a kiss.

"Exactly." He leaned down and granted my wish, lighting my heart on fire in the process.

Chapter 11

We walked back into the house holding hands, but the mood in the room had grown tense.

"What's up?" I asked, moving toward the table as Rob and Grace hovered over the largest book we'd retrieved from the safe.

"Come look at this. It's..." Rob paused and shook his head.

"Scary as hell," Grace finished his thought, and pushed the book across the table to me and Michael.

An image of the dark angel hovering just above the trees caught my attention first. A Grollic in the throes of transition sat before him, bent over in the agony of becoming human again, or perhaps wolf. I couldn't tell which way he was morphing due to the point at which the picture was painted.

"What does the dark angel have to do with the Grollics?" Michael reached out and brushed his fingers over the wolf.

"He's their creator," I mumbled, knowing I would receive a few shocked looks, but it was time to divulge all I knew, "and that's not just any wolf. It's Bentos. He couldn't shift because he was the seventh son of the seventh. He found out he could control Grollics but it wasn't enough."

"How do you know that?" Grace asked, her eyes wide and face flushed.

"I met an old woman in the forest on my last journey across the United States. She was a Grollic much like me, but incredibly old. She told me the story of the dark angel and the Grollics. Bentos wanted power more than anything else and the angel, in his mercy, gave it to him, but with power comes a price." I looked up.

"What was the price for dad's power?" Rob asked.

"The curse of the seventh son." I pressed my hands to the table, staring at the picture a little while longer. "I'm the curse presently."

"But you're not a son." Rob pointed out the obvious and got a sarcastic response from Michael.

"Brilliant observation, Rob."

"Shut the hell up," Rob barked at him.

"Hey. Enough, guys." I stood and moved back a little. "The woman said that the seventh child couldn't be a girl."

"But you're right here." Grace lifted her hand as confusion swept across her face.

"I know. She said if the curse were upon a female that the end was near." I bit my lip, not wanting to bring doom and gloom into the conversation, but not really having another choice. The truth was the truth.

"The end of what exactly?" Michael reached out and touched the back of my arm.

"Of the Grollics." I leaned back over and started to read the ornate writing beneath the image. "Oh... wow."

"Exactly." Rob took a seat and pressed his elbows to the table. "I assume you're to the part that says anyone who ingests the blood of the dark one will live no more?"

I glanced up. "Yeah, but who would willingly drink Mal..."

"Stop!" Michael shouted next to me.

"Sorry," I responded, pursing my lips at my almost slip up. "Who would drink his blood on purpose? That's disgusting."

"Would it kill anyone?" Michael asked, taking the seat next to me and moving closer.

"It says anyone." I looked over at him.

"Which would include your father." Grace stretched her hands out on the table and tapped the top of the book. "So we get the blood of the dark angel, force it down his throat and he dies."

We all stared at her in shocked silence. She acted like we were making a pie or putting together a desk. Add part a to part b and voila! Done.

"Not sure it's that easy." I glanced back down in hopes of it actually spelling out how one would go about getting the blood of the dark angel.

"But in theory, that's how it works. Right?" Her voice held a hint of defensiveness.

"Yes. That's exactly how it works, baby." Rob moved toward her and wrapped an arm around her shoulders. "It's just a little more complex in real life because, well because..."

Michael cut in, his voice no nonsense. "Because how the hell are you going to get the blood of a dark angel? I assume he goes by other names, maybe Lucifer?" He snorted. "They're probably cousins."

I rolled my eyes. "I've seen him face to face. He's not to be messed with. Not at all." I pushed the book away as a shiver ran down the center of my soul "He's pure evil. He helps and expects much in way of payment."

"What kind of payment are we talking about here, Rouge?" Rob looked up at me.

"A life. One that matters significantly to you." I brushed my hand over my face. "We'll not be asking for his blood. We need to figure out how to take it. That's our only hope."

"Take it? Are you out of your mind?" Rob laughed and sat back. "No way. That's a suicide mission. We need to bargain with him."

"No!" My tone was sharp and I narrowed my eyes on my brother. "You have no idea what you're dealing with."

"Then tell us." Rob leaned forward, giving me back what I was serving up.

I let out a long sigh and got up from the table. "I already did, Rob. He's evil at the core of its existence. He's darkness, death, pestilence, pain, suffering... all wrapped up in a near perfect bundle."

Michael jerked his head around as his eyes narrowed. "You've seen his face."

"Yes. Several times. You didn't at the beach that day?" I reached out and ran my hands over Michael's thick shoulders.

"No. He was just a shadow, though I could feel the darkness that you speak of. Horrible feeling actually." He let out a long exhale. "I don't want any of us hurt. Maybe there is another way around this."

"Let's keep searching in these journals and if we don't find anything, then we'll have you call Caleb." I squeezed Michael's shoulders and released him.

"What? That's a horrible idea!" Rob shot to his feet.

"Do you have a better one?" I turned on him, ready for a fight if he wanted to step on the dance floor with me. "I didn't say we were going to invite him to help us or to return to him, Rob. I said we would call for information. We're fighting their damn fight for them."

"Rouge has a point." Grace looked up toward Rob. "We are helping them. Whether they are our new enemy number one, we're fighting the same fight as they are. They might come to their senses and realize that helping us is their best bet in winning this war."

"Whatever." Rob walked out of the living room and down the hall.

"I can't blame him. The bastard betrayed us, drugged him and killed your mother." Michael stood and turned to face me. "Let's go on what you have for now, search more and as a last ditch effort call Caleb."

I nodded and walked down the hall to find my brother. I knew Grace wanted to go, but she wouldn't be able to bring him to understand where we were and where we needed to go like I would. We were on the precipice of bringing this battle to closure. I could feel it in my bones, and I was scared as hell.

I stopped by the door and tapped on the frame.

Rob glanced up from the bed and shook his head. "No. I don't like it. They're not going to get the opportunity to hurt us again, Jamie. They f—they lied, and you know it." He caught himself from swearing, probably for my sake, or knowing Rob, because of the baby growing in my belly.

"I know." I walked into the room and sat down beside him as he stiffened.

"Then why are you agreeing with this like it's our only option? It's not." He looked over at me with a pleading in his eyes that I couldn't deny.

"I'll protect us all if something goes wrong. You have to trust me." I reached out and took hold of his forearm. "You weren't there when things went down. I saved all of us and I came to save you."

"At what cost? Mom died, you lost a huge chunk of your innocence and Grace and Michael lost their guardians." He shook his head. "I know I'm just the mutt of the group, but if I get a vote at all—"

I cut him off. "You're not just the mutt of anything. You're my brother and I would have moved heaven and hell to get you back. When you died..."

I lost the volume to my voice as pain laced the center of me. A soft sob left me and I pressed my hands to my face. "I lost mom and then I thought I lost you."

Rob's voice was soft and thick with unshed tears too. "Hey. I'm sorry." He pulled me into a sideways hug and pressed his cheek to my head. "Don't cry, please?"

"I can't help it. I'm trying to figure this thing out, and we really don't have many options." I sat up and lifted my t-shirt, drying my tears and trying to get a hold of myself. "We can look through these journals, but it would be really great to talk to someone who knew the history and had the answers."

"And you think that's Caleb?"

"Well, it's not dear-old-dad." I gave him a look and sniffled.

He laughed, breaking the tension between us. "All right. I'll do my best to trust your judgment, but don't expect me to just sit by and let things fall apart again. I'm more vicious than the three of you put together, unless caught off guard and drugged. Then I'm useless."

I stood and offered him a hand. "Stop running from me and start looking for options with me. I don't trust Caleb and Sarah either, and neither does Michael, but they are our best bet for intel that rings true."

"Okay." He took my hand and pulled hard, forcing me to land on the bed beside him as he stood and jogged out in the hall. "Stop laying around. We have two evil bastards to slay. Gah... Women."

I rolled my eyes and stood, realizing that I was in the room that Joshua and I had spent several nights together in. The feelings inside of me weren't devastation over losing a man that I was in love with, but intense sadness over losing someone that was sure to be a part of my family.

"I'm sorry," I whispered and walked out of the room. I'd not only failed the alpha wolf, but murdered him against my own will as well. It was something I wasn't sure I could ever get over.

Michael walked in from outside as I moved into the living room and took a seat on the couch. Rob got busy starting a fire and soon Grace plopped down on the spot next to me, snuggling into my side and brushing her hand over my tummy.

"What're you going to name him?" She glanced up at me.

"How do you know it's a boy?" I smirked. "It might very well be a pretty little girl."

"I just have a feeling this first one's going to be a blond-haired, blue-eyed boy."

"So a heartbreaker?" I reached down and took her place, rubbing my stomach.

"Something like that." She rested against me and for a moment everything felt as if it might be okay.

"I just spoke with Caleb." Michael walked into the living room and sat down in my father's chair.

The moment was gone and reality settled back in.

"And?" I asked, working to keep my voice calm.

"I explained some of the situation that we're facing, but left out parts that I didn't feel that they needed to know." He ran his fingers through his hair and turned to Rob as my brother jerked around.

"And what parts was that?"

"That part where we're planning on figuring out how to shift the Grollics' life source from Bentos to Rouge before we kill him." Michael stiffened as if he were in the mood to fight too.

I lifted my hand in the air, which forced Grace to move back.

"Stop it, you two! We don't need them to know our plans at all. What we need is information on what they know about killing Bentos. We need to know what they know about the dark angel and that's it! We can take care of the rest." I scooted to the edge of my seat and turned my attention to Michael. "Right?"

"Exactly." He pursed his lips for a minute. "They're willing to share information with us, but they want to do it in person."

"No!" Rob stood and turned to face us.

"Rob. Please?" I glanced up at him with a look that hopefully reminded him of our conversation not ten minutes before.

"I told Caleb that only he and Sarah could come, no one else from the Higher Coven and that if they tried anything at all, that I would slay them both where they stood. Family or not."

Michael leaned back, his posture leaving me no doubt as to the heaviness that sat on him.

"And what did Caleb say?" Grace whispered.

"That he understood. He would not betray us again. They realize the error of what they did and want to rectify it."

"Bullshit," Rob barked.

"If they come here and anything happens, I'll show absolutely no mercy at all. You understand that, right?" I asked softly. I didn't have the power to control them or stop them. But I could control any Grollics around me and I would spend the rest of my life hunting Caleb down.

"I do. I believe Caleb has a lot to share with us, and where you cannot expect him to be warm and engaging with you and Rob, you can expect him to be respectful and willing to help." Michael glanced toward Grace. "You okay with them coming?"

"As long as they know the rules of engagement, of course." Grace stood and crossed her arms over her chest. "I'm not interested in a relationship with them, Michael. Don't expect a big family make-up time. That's not happening."

"I agree." Michael nodded. "I'm not making up with anyone myself, just looking for ways to protect my family going forward. You guys are all that matter to me."

My heart swelled in my chest as Michael turned and pinned me and Grace with recognition that we were his family, but it was when he nodded to my brother that I melted. I would love him forever and stand beside him for eternity.

"This will be neutral ground while we're here, so all I can ask is that while you don't have to be happy about them being here, please don't antagonize the situation." He glanced purposely at Rob. "They're on edge just like we are. Caleb's tolerance level is not very high. He is used to people following orders from him." Michael stood and stretched his hands toward the ceiling. "It's not the best of situations, but I think we'll work through it as long as Bentos doesn't make an appearance."

"I hope he does. We'll take a stand against him. All of us. Together." Rob spoke his commitment softly, but all of us heard the ferocity and felt the truth of it in our spirits. We would stand together. With Caleb and Sarah. We had no choice.

I sighed. Since meeting Michael and Grace, I never thought there would come a day that we would be standing against Sarah. Her sweetness and loyalty was something I respected. I'd always been cautious about Caleb, yet somehow I trusted him. He held his power different than Bentos. He was by no means sweet, but he protected those close to him. I had once felt that protection and I hoped he would take me under his wing again. Me and Rob.

However, I was no longer that naive girl anymore. I carried power within me and Michael's child. If Caleb tried to hurt any of us, I would protect them by any means necessary.

Chapter 12

Two days later

I pored over the bag of journals while we waited for Caleb and Sarah to arrive. They were Bentos' journals, covering decades of time and stopping suddenly about two decades ago. I wondered if it had anything to do with my birth but did not mention the thought out loud. It didn't matter. The journals weren't dated. They must have all been purchased a long time ago but the ink, the wording and all that, transgressed with time. There was no proof Bentos had stopped writing in them twenty years ago, but somehow I knew he had. I didn't need proof. He might not have been there for my birth, but the moment I came into this world, he knew he would one day lose his power and it terrified him.

The truth of the situation was simple. Bentos could be destroyed and we knew how to get a hold of the one who had the key element. The dark spirit. The freaky-scary dude.

However, figuring out how to drain Bentos of his blood, or even hold him still was a whole different problem we needed to worry about. We needed the dark angel's blood and Bentos had the dark angel's blood now in him. We were sure of it.

After another restless sleep, I got up early and headed into the kitchen. Michael was absent from the bed, his spot where he had lain cool. Even my light sleep hadn't noticed him leave.

Rob stood by the sink, staring out in the distance as if lost in thought. He'd kept to himself lately, almost as if he were preparing for us to part ways soon. Like he didn't want to make it any harder on me than it had to be.

"Hey." I reached out and touched his shoulder.

He jerked around quickly as if scared. "Oh. Sorry... They're here."

"Caleb and Sarah?" I moved toward the window to see Michael and Grace undoing the boat on our side of the lake. Across the way, two lone figures stood, their faces not easily recognizable.

"Yeah. Let the fight—I mean fun—begin, right?" Rob snorted and moved to sit down at the kitchen table.

I watched the view outside a little longer, ignoring his jab and then turning, joined him at the table. We stared at each other. "We need to focus on how to get your lifeline off of Bentos'. Maybe onto me, or all Grollics onto me." I sighed heavily, feeling the weight of responsibility before it even belonged to me. "Or onto the dark angel if we have to." I'd have to find a way to bargain with the dark ghost himself...but at what price then?

"You think that's possible?"

"I hope so. I'm not sure we'll find it in any of these stupid books though." I reached out and ran my fingers over the nearest pile of them. "I wonder if the original journal I have would hold any additional information." I'd gone through it so many times, and yet it seemed to constantly surprise me with information I never noticed before, like it magically appeared.

"Maybe. It's worth another look." He leaned back in his chair and frowned as he stared out the window. "Use the need for some alone time later and sneak away to check it out."

I nodded, agreeing with his plan. "This is going to suck, isn't it?" Nerves settled in my belly and I resisted the urge to shudder.

"Pretty sure. They tried to kill us less than a week ago. Now we're inviting them to stay in the same house with us." He let out a painful sigh. "I'm trusting you on this one."

"I know. I appreciate it." I stood and walked to the door, glancing over my shoulder and giving him a tight smile. "I'll not let you down. I promise."

"Something in me believes that more than I should." He smiled back.

Turning, I opened the door and walked out into the yard and down to the lake. Grace stood by the shore, her shoulders rigid and expression deadpan. Michael was across the lake, helping Caleb and Sarah get into the boat.

"I don't like it. I really don't." Grace looked over at me. "It's such a painful feeling to not want them here. They taught us everything we know, sheltered and protected us. Caleb had plans for me to mate with another hunter. To give my Sioghra away. I never did... I couldn't."

"You were waiting for Rob."

She blinked and stared at me. "I haven't given him mine." She touched the pendant under her shirt. "I should have, don't you think? To show them I'm with Rob."

"That's not why you would give it to Rob."

She pressed her mouth into a thin line. "It's just so confusing."

"I know." I wrapped my arm around the back of her shoulders and tried to focus on my own feelings.

I felt nothing but peace at the moment. My body was telling me we were doing the right thing. I had to trust my instincts, they would sense danger. I knew better back in Port Coquitlam than to go to Caleb's, but I wanted to support Michael. He believed in Caleb so deeply, I wanted to as well.

His feeling of betrayal had cut us all deeper than we could have imagined.

After Bentos was dead and the dark angel gone, it would be time to start a new life. One where being a hunter or a Grollic didn't matter. All that counted would be loving each other and raising our baby. I refused to call it a boy, or a girl, just yet. Part of me didn't want to call it anything, just in case something happened to me... I pushed the silly thought aside, refusing to listen to my fear.

"Grace. Catch this." Michael lifted a rope and launched it at us. It dropped on the wooden dock by Grace's feet, but she didn't budge.

"I'll get it." I moved quickly, scooping it up and pulling them toward the dock as Grace turned and walked back up to the house without a word. If anyone understood her pain, it was me. My mother had abandoned me at birth and my father had tried to kill me more times than I could count.

"Thanks, Rouge." Michael moved past Sarah and helped me tie the boat to the dock. He moved off the boat and helped Sarah as I stepped back. I wasn't thrilled to see them either, but I refused to make matters worse.

"Rouge," Sarah spoke quietly and nodded toward me.

"Thanks for coming. I think you'll find what we've uncovered quite interesting, but you may already know everything we've discovered." I spoke with little to no emotion to my voice. Not by choice, but necessity. Anger would have burned brightly inside of me at simply seeing Caleb's face, but there was a greater good to be served by sitting at the table with my enemies.

"Perhaps. Maybe not." Caleb moved toward me with a look of regalia on his face. He was supreme compared to me and his expression screamed that reality.

"We'll see, I guess." I took Michael's hand as he offered it and walked up the hill with them in tow.

"Let's get everyone around the table and walk them through what we know and then we'll ask our questions." Michael looked over at me as if asking for my compliance.

"Sure. It's a good place to start." I glanced back and kept my eyes on Sarah. "Any objections?"

"I want a moment with Michael and Grace first," Caleb barked, moving over to get into my line of vision.

"Not happening." Michael opened the door to the house. "Play by our rules or get out and don't look back. Simple and straightforward."

Sarah nodded and walked into the house, going to the kitchen and sitting next to Rob.

My brother stiffened, but didn't show an ounce of disdain.

I moved to sit beside him with Grace on the other side of me. The others filed around the table and I opened the first book, not waiting for the silence to get any more awkward. "We found these journals in the basement here. We've discovered that one means of killing Bentos is to gain access to the blood of a dark angel that's started to rear his ugly head." I pushed the book toward Caleb and Sarah, but only she glanced down. Caleb watched me with interest.

"The dark angel doesn't just show up. You have called upon him." He clasped his hands on the table in front of him.

"And you're familiar with this beast?" Rob asked, his tone pinched. "A brother perhaps?"

I kicked Rob under the table as a warning. He rolled his eyes at me.

Caleb ignored Rob's sarcastic comment. "I am familiar. Mostly because I've been around a long time." Caleb turned his focus back to me. "You've called him to aid you." The disgust dripped from his words.

"Yes, but he came to me the first two times before I realized I had access to him."

"Impossible," Sarah said quietly as Caleb pursed his lips.

"Believe what you want, but he came to me and Michael in a shared dream, I was here and Michael was..."

"With the hunting party with the two of you in the mountains just outside of here," Michael finished and reached out and took the book from me. "The point is... we believe this creature has the power to kill Bentos."

"Of course he does. He created him. Bentos is not the first seventh son. He's just the first to harness the darkness along with it." Caleb sat back in his chair. "You'll never get a hold of the darkness. He's too powerful for that. He's the morning star, Michael. The greatest and oldest evil known to this earth."

"Who else is he to you, Caleb?" Michael leaned forward, pinning his mentor with a hard stare.

"Don't ask questions you're not ready to hear the answer to." Caleb crossed his arms over his chest and turned back to me. "So you have a weapon, though it's not the only one. There are several others to my knowledge."

"Are you referring to the strength or power of three?" I had to ask. If we were laying everything out on the table, then I was prepared to give up my secrets too. I wanted an end to the madness and this seemed to be a way to get it. Collective effort and perseverance to go to the depths of hell if necessary.

I wanted peace.

Caleb nodded, his poker face beautifully locked in place. "That is another, though no one knows what that truly means."

I wanted to scream. Rob had known about it, Michael apparently had been told by Caleb. Did Grace know about it as well? How could everyone know, but me, and still not understand what it was.

"Tell us what you think the three items are," Grace finally spoke and I was glad to see Caleb's expression soften a little toward my best friend.

"It's a prophecy from the Grollics, which says that close to the end of time, a creature will hold the strength of three, which has the power to bring down all entities that come against it, especially the Grollic Master." He glanced down at his hands and shook his head. "I don't believe it. It's a tale. Power corrupts. That would be almost too much for anyone, Grollic, hunter or human. None are meant to control it all." His head popped up and his eyes rested on me when he said the last sentence.

"You don't think Bentos could handle all the power?" I ignored the assumption directed toward me.

"Not at all. He's been driven to the brinks of insanity by his maker as it is right now. We're going to take him out first and then attack the dark angel. Simply taking out one and not the other is half finishing the job. It makes no sense." He let out a quick puff of air. "To be completely honest, either of them would love for us to do their dirty work for them."

"What do you mean?" Michael asked.

Sarah spoke up, her voice firm, but soft. "If one dies, the other gains strength."

"So right now they share their power? The source of their strength?" Rob leaned in, his eyes going wide with interest.

"Yes, but it's shared between them... and her." Caleb nodded to me. "Actually, I believe she's tilting the scales."

Chill bumps ran down my arms and covered my legs. Surely he was wrong. I felt like a weakling against both my father and this dark angel who tossed me about to and fro like I weighed nothing. "How so?"

"The other night at our house, I've never seen anything like what you did." Caleb ran his hands over his face and shook his head. "If it wasn't done in the name of evil, I'd be beyond impressed."

"It was survival." I leaned forward, gritting my teeth together. "I'm not evil."

"That's what you want to believe." Caleb didn't bat an eye.

"Watch yourself," Michael growled at his mentor.

"Fine." Caleb dropped his hands on his lap, appearing quite unimpressed with our angst. "You have more power than you know, Rouge. I would say that whatever we decide, it'll be you or I who have to go into the fray and cause the damage."

"Go together." Sarah reached out and touched Caleb's arm.

"Not a good idea. I still don't trust you. I'd be watching my back because of you and Bentos."

"As I would," Caleb retorted.

"I didn't start this war." My voice rose, angry that he had blamed me from the start. "You sent Michael to find me. You had wanted him to kill me that night in the graveyard when we met. You had no idea I carried hunter blood inside of me."

Caleb glared at me. "His weakness is my mistake."

Rob growled.

Caleb waved his hand as if pushing a dog away from the table. "He didn't and so I tried to use what I could of my knowledge of you to do something right. You have the power to destroy all Grollics. If it means killing yourself in the process and breaking my son's heart, so be it. That was a risk I was willing to take."

"I'm not dispensable. Michael would never have agreed to that."

"He didn't!" Caleb's voice rose. "No matter how many times I tried to convince him of what you were. He refused to believe. Now I find myself without the twins." He blinked suddenly and cleared his throat, glaring at me. "Without my understudy, Grace with whom should be with another hunter, but instead is caught up in the webs of your brother's snare, my eternal partner is angry with me and the Higher Coven is at the brink of war with themselves! All because of you, Rouge! So forgive me if I do not share the kindness you feel should be extended to you." He snapped his teeth together. "You've taken everything from me and now are allowed this abomination to grow inside your belly. You think that thing is a child? It is nothing more than a beast. The dark angel will take it, harness its powers and fill this world with darkness! Have you stopped to consider that?"

No one spoke, all of us too shocked at his words.

Caleb snorted. "So now I am forced to play the hand of the servant and do your bidding. I must go against everything I have fought for all my life! You say you don't trust me, well I sure as hell don't trust you!" He snapped up one of the journals. "So what are your plans, children? How are you going to fight this war with your little tin soldiers and plastic guns? What are your plans?"

"You think I chose this life?"

"None of us did, Rouge." Caleb's eyes burned bright blue. "That's the whole point."

"You have a retort for everything, don't you?" Anger seeped through my words and I needed to calm down. We needed to work together and fighting with Caleb was only going to make this impossible. I took a deep breath and let it out slowly. "We need to set our differences aside, Caleb. We don't have a choice but to work together." I stood. "I'm going to step outside." I patted Michael's hand as he reached for me. "I'm okay. I just need a moment. I think we all do. We need to focus on how we're going to capture the blood of the dark angel."

"He'll have to be killed if that's your plan, Rouge, and that's not possible." Caleb's voice followed me as I walked to the back door. I paused to pick up my journal, but didn't respond. I was happy to hear Michael do it for me.

"Then we'll have to come up with a new plan. Something has to give here. We're running in circles. Rouge is doing everything she can to find a way to stop this."

I walked from the cabin, not realizing I was stomping until I stepped on a medium-size branch and it cracked from the pressure of my foot. Tucking the warming journal under my arm, I headed into the forest with expedience but forced my step to lighten.

"Show me the truth," I whispered and closed my eyes as I paused by a large oak tree. The air in front of me shimmered and a bright light darted across the pathway just ahead of me. I half expected it to be Malaz, but the light wasn't his style at all.

I moved toward the fluttering light and lost its movement as the wind picked up.

"Show yourself!" I demanded, swinging my eyes left to right as the hair on the back of my neck rose.

Rebekah.

Wait, what?!

"Rouge, my darling. I wanted so badly to check on you and Rob." She crossed her hands in front of her waist and tilted her head, studying me.

"I'm so sorry," I whispered roughly, not expecting to encounter her. How was that even possible? It felt like I was dreaming, not really standing in the forest staring at what looked like a ghost and talking to it.

"I chose my end, child. I just wanted you to know that I'm here."

"Shouldn't you... you know, be gone?" I glanced around, trying to make sure we were alone.

"I can't." She looked as if she wanted to say something and then stopped herself. She smiled. "It is better this way. I can keep a watch on you and Rob."

"Are you his mother?" I took a step toward her as my heart ached in my chest.

She blinked in surprise, as if the question was a ridiculous one. "Of course I am." She moved toward me, reaching out and touching the side of my face.

Tears filled my eyes. I couldn't feel her touch. There would never be an opportunity to truly feel the warmth of her hug now that she was gone.

"Why did Rob not die back at the warehouse?" I pressed my hand to the outside of hers, but only touched my own cheek.

"He did." She moved back, her smile warm and endearing.

"Are you sure? His eyes didn't change color."

She glanced around as fear brushed across her face. "I have to go. Get back to the house."

"What? Why?" I took a step toward her, but she screamed and pulled back farther and farther until she was gone.

"Rebekah!" I ran toward her only to be stopped in my tracks. "Mom! Wait—"

The dark angel moved toward me with slow calculated steps and a smirk on his impossibly beautiful mouth.

"Why do you seek my destruction child? Am I not the creator of your people?" He tilted his head as his crystal black eyes roamed across my face.

"I didn't call you here." I started to shake at the realization that I wasn't at all prepared for whatever he was doing in front of me.

"No one calls me to their presence. I am the bane of darkness. Why would you think I am beckoned by a mere child?" He moved so fast, I didn't have time to react. His fingers slid into my hair and he tightened what felt like a claw around my head.

I cried out and hated the sound of my weakness.

He seemed to read my thoughts and took pleasure in the ones that brought me fear. "I will help you kill your father, but you must do something in return for me."

"What?" I whispered, feelings of terror, horror, fear, dread, and disgust coursing through my veins. I hated his touch, it made me want to throw up. A sudden thought hit me like a slap in the face. "I will not give you my—"

A wicked smile lifted his muted pink lips, cutting me off. "Take his place."

Chapter 13

I heard Rob yelling, but couldn't figure out what he was shouting about. I had to focus on Malaz. I'd not let him touch Rob, or Grace, or anyone I loved.

Jerking away from him, time slowed momentarily as he moved backward as if in slow motion, retreating deeper into the forest before disappearing.

I had no doubt that I would see him again. Soon.

"No. It's their fault she's dead!" Rob's voice was loud and full of unsent anger.

I turned on my heel and raced toward the house. I couldn't get back fast enough. "What's going on?" I skidded to a stop beside my brother and Grace, as she seemed to be trying to get him to calm down.

"Caleb brought up the scene at the facility and said that they lost a lot of people." Grace gave me a quick look that pleaded for help.

"It was the tone he used," he growled at Caleb. "We wouldn't have had to fight for our lives had you not sent them after us, had you not kidnapped me!"

I put my hand on Rob's shoulder trying to calm him.

He shrugged me off, but did lower his voice slightly. "Like we didn't lose anyone. My mother died in that fight trying to save me and Rouge, because unlike you people, she has a heart." Rob's words were beyond harsh and Grace jerked back as if he'd slapped her.

"I'm not like them," she whispered as tears filled her eyes. "But you can't see that right now, can you?"

"Grace." He reached for her, but she spun around and ran out of the room.

Rob ran his fingers through his messy mop of hair and turned to me, growling loudly, "Why can't anything work out?"

"Because tensions are high and we have to rely on our enemies to give us direction and help. It's a sticky place to be in." I shoved my hands in the pockets of my jeans. "Give her a bit of time and then go apologize. Her and Michael are exactly like Rebekah was, if not more so."

"I know." He growled again. "Shit. I know."

I glanced behind me, wondering if I should tell him about seeing Rebekah and Malaz.

"Did you have any luck out there?" He nodded to the journal in my hands.

I glanced down and shook my head. "No. I kept hearing things, seeing things."

"You want me to go back out there with you and maybe we can look together through the journal?"

He needed someone to be around that didn't leave his skin crawling. That was me. I held back telling him about seeing Rebekah and what Malaz wanted from me.

"Yeah. I'd like that actually." I turned toward the forest and started back up the hill with Rob next to me.

"It's just you and me sis." He put his arm around me and let out a quick sigh. "You really think the dark angel's blood could kill Bentos?"

I nodded, swallowing at the sudden dryness in my throat. "I'm pretty sure I can get Bentos to come. Trapping him might be a different story." I tucked away the information that Malaz had plans for me. Plans I would never in a million years agree to. I'd sooner die than become my father or Malaz's lap dog.

"Let's check in the journal to see if there's anything in there we can use against him. Didn't you say one time that there were drawings that showed a Grollic's weaknesses? Maybe there's one about the dark dumbass too?"

"Dark dumbass?" I laughed, despite the heaviness of the situation we were in. "I don't know where you come up with this stuff Rob. I wish we'd have grown up together. It'd have been a laugh."

He hugged me with the arm still around my shoulders. "I wasn't the nicest guy. Didn't do all the right things. You'd have probably hated me."

"Or maybe, if Rebekah hadn't had to hide from Bentos, I wasn't the seventh mark and been given away in hiding, we might have had a cool life." I pulled the journal from under my arm and held it up, preferring to not think about what could have beens. "I honestly can't imagine there being anything in here for the simple fact that Bentos would have used it already. Malaz has to be his greatest threat." I stopped by a large walnut tree, glanced around and moved to sit down on the chilly forest floor.

Rob dropped down and laid on his side, pulling at dead grass and staring off into space.

I opened the journal, taking advantage of him being quiet for a minute to see what I could find.

The pages fluttered back and forth as if the wind were blowing them. I pulled my hand back and let the book land where it would. Power brushed by me and I glanced up to see if Rob was paying attention. He wasn't. He was frozen in time, his eyes wide and face slack.

"What the hell?" I whispered and looked down at a page with writing that went blank. Then words began to appear slowly from the bottom to the top, right to left. I had to wait until the entire thing was on display to understand what it wanted of me.

It is with new life that the old things will pass away and the new will gain life. In the essence of angelic existence lies the key to destroy the dark one. One will come who will hold the power of both the heavens and the earth. Only then will the dark one find himself trapped by two greater powers than his evil has ever created. Only then will the child be able to harness the strength of three. And with that gift... the end will begin.

The air seemed frozen suddenly. I couldn't breathe. Clarity would soon be mine and the end of the Grollics would be within reach. The thought excited and horrified me all in the same moment. I gasped for breath when my lungs threatened to explode.

Rob's voice scared me and I jumped.

"Why are you crying?" He rolled to his knees, reaching out and brushing a tear from my cheek.

"I didn't know I was." I wiped at the other side of my face and handed him the book. "Read this if you can."

He took the book and dropped it, jerking back with a yelp. "Damn. It's blazing hot. Very funny, Jamie."

"*Rouge*, and I forgot it's hot to your touch." I picked it up and started to work through the contents again.

"How about you read it to me, or at least tell me what you're thinking."

I stared down at the page, half expecting it to change back to the original wording but it didn't. "I'm not sure about the first line, but the second one references the essence of angelic existence being the key to destroying the dark one, who I assume is the dark angel or spirit."

"What's the reference of essence of angelic existence?" Rob sat back on his heels and gave me a look of confusion. "That's a friggin' mouthful."

I tugged Michael's Sioghra out from under my shirt and wrapped my fingers around it. "I think it's this... the angel's lifeblood."

"So the angel's blood will kill the dark one. Good. Send Caleb. Hopefully the scary bastard gives the snooty king of the angels something to think about." Rob growled then shrugged as I gave him a warning look. "What? I hate that guy."

"It says that one will come that holds the power of both heaven and earth."

"Earth or hell?" Rob moved closer, but kept his hands to himself.

"Earth." I sucked my lip into my mouth and glanced up. "The power of heaven and earth."

"Heaven could be the hunters and earth could be the Grollics."

I looked up and chuckled. "That's it. Brilliant. So it's someone that is both angel and Grollic."

"So either of us." Rob lifted his eyebrow and smiled.

"Right, but I'm the only one with a Sioghra, although, I feel like you should have one too. The fact that you don't worries the heck out of me." I glanced back down at the book, comfortable with the fact that it was referring to me. I was certain it was going to be me going after Malaz anyway.

"Being both Grollic and hunter is enough to trap him, or so this says."

"What else?" Rob moved closer, letting his knees press to mine as he sat down fully on the ground.

"Only then will the child be able to harness the strength of three. And with that gift... the end will begin." I closed the book and took in a deep breath. "Whatever the dark angel gives up to me, it opens the doorway not only for us to see what the strength of three is, but it also brings about the end of the Grollics."

Rob's eyes shifted down and he nodded. "Good. Then it's the way things are supposed to work out."

"No. I don't believe that." I reached out and touched his knee. "I'll figure out how to work all of this out, but first things first. I have a date with the greatest evil earth's known."

I got up and dusted off my pants. Scared crap-less but at least we had something—a bit of a plan. Destiny was opening slowly and offering me the next steps in finishing this fight. I felt ready for the after party. It was coming.

"I'm glad you feel like you validated the fact that it's you that has to go after this evil being, but I still don't get how you're going to kill him."

"Great feats require great sacrifice," I quoted some movie or book I remembered hearing. I lifted Michael's Sioghra again and watched the garnet red essence inside sparkle as I held it up toward the late afternoon sunlight. "I need my lifeblood back. I'll get close to the dark angel, slash him with it, and hope for the best."

"Um, right..." Rob looked over at me as we walked down the hill together. "And don't you need that blood to keep you alive and walking around here on the earth?"

"Yep, but not all of it." I shrugged. "That part I need to check with Caleb."

"Oh great! Count me out. I've had all I can handle of Mr. High and Mighty Arse today."

I laughed and stopped by the back door. "I'll talk to them with Michael. You go find Grace and tell her you're sorry."

"For what?" His smirk told me he knew exactly what he was apologizing for.

"For being an ass." I winked and walked into the house.

The tension had grown so thick it felt like I might need a blade to cut my way to the kitchen table. Caleb and Sarah sat on one side and Michael on the other. The look on my boyfriend's face told me things weren't progressing. The journals lay basically untouched on the table.

"Rouge. You okay?" Michael awarded me with a tight smile.

"I'm fine. I found out something about getting close to the dark angel and harnessing his power." I moved to sit by Michael and made sure to focus on Caleb. "Tell me something..."

"What?" He leaned forward, pressing his forearms to the table.

"If a hunter loses some of the blood from their Sioghra, what happens?"

"You mean if it spills?" Michael asked and scooted closer to me. He reached out and rubbed his hand along my back, the action comforting, but most likely a reminder to the people across the table that he and I were a united front.

"You would weaken," Caleb answered, his voice deadpan. "It's damn near impossible to get the Sioghra to open. It's a learned trick."

"Teach me." I leaned forward too, not at all intimidated by the man across from us, though perhaps I should have been.

"Why?" Sarah asked, her voice soft and much less abrasive than Caleb's.

"Because my journal states that I'm the one that can capture the dark angel's essence to take out Bentos." I leaned back, tiring already from playing a game of who's got the bigger stick.

"I can see that happening." Caleb lifted his fingers to his mouth and brushed them over his lips as he watched me. "When are you thinking of trying this?"

"She's not." Michael turned toward me with anger on his face. "You're not going to take on this dark evil by yourself. It's suicide. It's crazy and irrational."

"And the only way I can find that leaves us holding the one weapon that will take my father out fully." I turned back to Caleb. "Teach me or you send me out there without a weapon. I'm working to bring Bentos to his end. It's what you want and we do too."

"And what about your brother? Ready to see him perish as well?" Caleb asked, his tone losing strength as if some part of him felt bad for the situation before me.

"Teach me how to open the Sioghra. Please." I stood and nodded toward the door. "Now."

He stood as well and looked down at Sarah, concern brushing across his handsome face. "You and Michael stay here. We won't be long."

"No. I'm coming." Michael stood and moved toward me, but I lifted my hand to stop him.

"No. Give me the necklace and hold onto yours as I work this out. I'll be right back and Caleb won't hurt me." I looked over to Caleb. "Will you?"

"No. I swear it on Sarah's life." Caleb turned to Michael. "Stay here with Sarah, please. I don't want her alone."

She laughed and looked up at Michael. "He still thinks I need protection, though I could whoop him in a fight any day."

A smile played at the edge of Michael's mouth and I was glad to see it. Maybe not all was lost. He looked over at me and let his eyes move around my face as if memorizing me.

"You sure you'll be okay?" He reached up and took the necklace off. "Keep mine with you, okay?"

"I'll be fine." I took my necklace and put it around my neck, carefully laying it on top of his.

"Let's go." Caleb walked to the door and opened it before moving outside and holding the door for me.

I walked out and closed the door. "I thought you said it was a learned trick and virtually impossible."

"It is for most, but not for you." He nodded toward the open field behind the house. "Let's go out a little ways and I'll teach you the meditation that will open it. Most hunters aren't strong enough to open their Sioghra. The magic that holds it closed is far more powerful than you might think."

I pulled mine up and memorized the beautiful engravings on it. To know that my body made it was something else.

There was no fear inside of me as Caleb turned toward me and closed his eyes, letting out a deep breath.

"Close your eyes and imagine what the heavens might look like. Settle your soul and when you have... a light will appear.

Take hold of it and open the container that holds it. Once you do, you've successfully broken the power on your Sioghra. Most people never see the light. Let's see how special you really are."

I ignored the challenge in his voice and closed my eyes, letting the world go and rushing toward the brilliance of how I imagined forever to be.

Chapter 14

Soft white mist gathered around my legs, but a solid pebble pathway sat beneath my feet. I glanced around and smiled. The trees surrounding me were large and filled to the brim with brilliant colored leaves. It was autumn in heaven and the scene was majestic. I breathed in deeply and settled my soul, calm becoming a quick companion for my journey.

A bright light moved toward me at a relaxed rate and by the time it reached me, I was more than ready to receive it. Extending my hands, I took it into my grasp and lifted the small trinket toward my face. The sterling silver appearance shone so brightly that it threatened to blind me with its radiance.

The heart-shaped trinket had a clasp that was accessible along the side. I pulled at it and opened the shell. A heart-shaped vile of red liquid lay protected inside of it. The cap at the top seemed to slip off without much effort but once it did, my energy weaned.

"Come back to me, Rouge." I could hear Caleb's voice, but it was incredibly far away.

I closed the top, locked the outer cage and closed my eyes, willing myself back to the cabin in Colorado.

When I opened my eyes again, I was kneeling in front of Caleb, my breathing labored and my skin covered in a sheen of sweat.

"You did it." He bent down in front of me, the look on his face that of fatherly pride. It didn't belong to me, but I enjoyed it for a moment anyway. No matter the devastation of what Caleb's relationship would become with Michael, I would forever covet what it had been. The love of a parent was something I'd never experienced, and never would. His anger against me seemed to have diminished... for now.

He reached for me and I took his hand, accepting his help as I stood.

"It was beautiful up there." I glanced down to find my Sioghra still intact right next to Michael's.

"I know. I go quite often to find my center." He crossed his arms over his chest, and for a moment seemed like a normal guy and not the monster he had become of late. "So when you find yourself in front of the dark angel, you know how to open yourself up. What we need now is someone or something to stun him so that you have time to access your lifeblood."

"Maybe there's something in my journal. Like a spell."

Caleb snapped his fingers. "There is! It's an ancient spell that uses the light to blind the darkness. Find it and memorize it." He snorted and shook his head. "This might actually work. Incredible. All these years we've been trying to use brute force to hunt and try to kill Bentos and yet I knew it would take so much more. We might actually win this time."

"We will." I tucked the necklaces back into my shirt. "If you're going back in, do you mind to send Michael out? I'm going to sit up on the hill for a while. See if I can find the spell and make it work."

"When are we planning on putting this new strategy into action? I say we don't wait. We go tonight."

"Tomorrow night." I brushed my hands over my stomach. "I need to rest before going through all of this."

He glanced down and his expression darkened, but he didn't give away any of his negative thoughts. Instead, he gave me a single nod then walked away.

I moved up the hill and sat down, stretching my legs out and leaning back to watch the sun work to finish up its task for the day. It would duck behind the clouds within minutes and leave the evening stars on display for all who took the time to see them. The ground was cool but I ignored it.

I looked down toward the house in time to watch Michael walk up the hill toward me. Butterflies tore up my stomach at the sight of him. His strong shoulders were pulled back, as if he could carry the weight of the world on them. His blond hair was getting a little too long, and was curling up around the edges like Rob's did on a daily basis.

"Hey, handsome." I smiled up at him as he dropped down next to me, moving close and staring seriously at me.

"I don't like it. You could get horribly hurt, Rouge. This isn't just about me and you anymore, but a child now too. If you die... he dies." He reached out and touched my stomach.

"It's going to work."

"I'm scared shitless and Sarah agrees with me. I told her about the baby and she thinks we need to find another way. Maybe one of us can do it. Why does it have to be you?" He moved his hand from my belly and turned to look out toward the horizon. "I'm going to do it. That's final."

I chuckled and slid my arm around his before pressing a soft kiss to his shoulder. "I wish it were that easy, Michael. But it's not. It has to be a hunter and Grollic mix. That's me and only me. It's my destiny to do this. Let me do it, and please support me while I do."

He looked over at me as emotions warred in his eyes. "I can't lose you, Rouge. You know that right? I can't."

"I know. You're not going to. We're forever, remember?"

"I think we should wait a while, before we do this. Take time to really think through how we're going to..."

I pressed my finger to his lips and smiled. "Tomorrow night. Stop trying to control this. It's going to work out beautifully. I can feel it."

"Right." He captured my hand and pressed kisses along my palm and up my arm. "I wish I could."

I pressed my fingers under his chin and lifted his face before moving in and brushing a soft kiss by his lips.

He groaned and slid his hands into my hair, pulling at me to sit in his lap as he deepened the kiss.

I complied and snuggled against him as he made love to my mouth, his actions sweet and sensual all at the same time.

He broke the kiss and brushed his nose by mine. "Soon we'll start celebrating forever."

"I'd like that." I took a shallow breath. "I hope that Caleb and Sarah won't attack us when this is all over. I promised you that I wouldn't hurt them, and I don't want to, but I'll defend our baby until the end against anyone... even you."

Michael brushed his hand over my swollen stomach and turned his gaze toward me. The brilliant blue of his eyes stole my breath. He was beyond beautiful and I was lost to him for as long as he would have me.

"I'll protect both of you until time ends. Don't worry about all that stuff, okay? We'll figure it out as we go. However... there is one thing I want cleared up before we go into this next round of fighting." He repositioned me on the ground next to him and moved to his knees in front of me.

Anxiety swept through me like a tidal wave and my eyes went wide as he pulled out a small black box.

"It's not much. Rob and I searched like hell at the little store a few days ago to find it, but anyway... Rouge, will you marry me? Make me yours and let us bring our son into the world with us joined as one?" The love in his eyes seared me to the center of my soul.

"Yes. Of course." I lifted a shaky hand and he slid the simple rose gold ring on it before pulling me into a hug and falling backward, leaving me half sprawled across the top of him as we kissed over and over again.

"Hey!" Grace's voice pulled us from our intimacy and Michael stole one more kiss before getting up and reaching for me. "Dinner's ready!"

I chuckled and started down the hill with him, but jerked to a stop as something whispered my name. *Rouge...*

"What is it?" Michael turned to look behind us for a moment.

"You heard that?" I asked, assuming he'd heard it too. I instinctively moved closer to him.

He wrapped his arm around my shoulder. "No. What?" He looked down at me as his brow furrowed. "Rob hollering?"

I pulled from him and smiled as we drew near the cabin. "Nothing. Just my wild imagination."

"Good. Come inside and let's feed my boy." Michael tugged at me.

"Sounds good." I pretended to smack my forehead. "Hold on. You go in, I'll be right there. I left my journal up on the hill."

"Want me to grab it?"

"Nah, I know exactly where it is. I'll be just a moment." I took a step back and forced a smile. "Don't let my brother eat everything before I get back."

"I'll fend him off and have a plate for you safely protected." He opened the door and paused. "Don't go into the woods, okay?"

"No worries." I watched him go in and turned, walking to the edge of the woods and stopping suddenly. "I'm here. What do you want?" My voice came out low and demanding.

"You, child. I want you." Malaz appeared a few yards from me, just inside the depths of the forest.

I took a step down the path and then another. An ancient chant I don't remember saying, let alone reading, bubbled up inside of me and spilled over. I didn't have time to analyze any of what was happening, but I stayed on my guard nonetheless.

Malaz's bottomless eyes widened as his mouth twisted in a silent cry. "Where did you learn that? Stop or I'll kill the child in your womb, girl."

I continued to walk toward him as the wind created a slow moving twister around him as he stood, stuck to the forest floor. I chanted the words over and over, the scene around me growing darker. I wasn't sure if it was from the sun setting or my sight once again changing color.

"Stop. Now!" he hissed, his voice growing louder. "I command you to stop! You've no idea what you're doing." He screamed so loudly something popped deep in my left ear and the warmth of liquid rushing over the side of my ear canal forced me to stop moving. The pain was incredible, but somehow lost to the insatiable need inside of me to keep the cadence of my foreign language steady.

He screamed again and I lurched back as my head jerked back, the feeling very much like someone punched me in the face. Liquid poured down my nose and my voice rose higher and higher.

The wind blew higher, covering my enemy and leaving the bottom of his dark gown on display. It was no longer fluid and alive, but had turned into casted black stone.

I closed my eyes and found my center, rushing into the throne room of heaven and reaching greedily for the light. I opened my Sioghra and forced myself back to the belly of the forest as the dark angel jerked and twitched violently.

"Damn you! This is not a game. I rescind the offer for you to take your father's place. NEVER! Your father will see you dead. I've given all of myself to him. He will destroy you for us."

I uncapped my lifeblood and jerked my wrist as the chant flowed from my lips again. Now was the time. I had no choice. The large tree next to me offered support as I reached over and pressed my free hand against it as instant weakness and exhaustion slammed into me.

Malaz screamed again. A horrible sound that echoed inside of me, leaving me feeling empty and forsaken. The wind around him consumed him, twirling like a small tornado spinning faster and faster. It uprooted small trees around us and dead leaves whipped across my face. I closed my eyes, trying to prevent dirt from getting into them.

I chanted continuously, the words foreign on my tongue, even as I repeated them over and over again. Forcing my eyes open to watch Malaz, I gasped. The strange wind and whatever else was inside of it had turned and twisted him into a stunning macabre statue. He looked like a magnificent black angel, his arms lifted high and heavy emotion on his perfectly sculpted face.

I jerked back as the wind shifted black as night and swept toward me. Like I was its next target.

"No! What's happening?" I cried out as it circled me, leaving me cold and unsettled. My back was pressed against the trunk of the large tree. I had nowhere to run or escape. "No! The curse was for him..."

The darkness slithered around my legs and circled my chest as I shrunk back terrified it would seep inside my skin and steal my baby. I let out a blood-curdling scream.

It wound around me in a tight circle until it was nothing but a small tendril of smoke. The wisp floated in the air above my chest, rising to eyelevel. Suddenly it hesitated its ascent and curled in a small circle before diving down in a mad rush. I barely had time to let out a scream, horrified it was going to cut me open and turn my heart and body into the marble statue beside me. It sped down, the small curled loop opened the top of my Sioghra and rushed inside. The last tendril of smoke wrapped around my wrist and forced me to close the cap and lock the heart trinket before disappearing.

I would die. The baby inside me would never survive this. I fell to my knees as the darkness consumed me from the inside out. Visions of death and carnage rushed by me and I screamed again, sounding like Malaz a moment earlier.

"Make it stop," I cried out and swatted as two strong hands wrapped around my upper arms. "Get away from me!"

"What's the matter with her?" I could hear Michael scream as I looked up through a haze of darkness into Caleb's face.

"Dammit! The dark angel's power mixed with hers." Caleb took me into his arms. "I've never seen eyes black as this... not since..." He tutted and began to jog out of the forest. "The next hours are crucial."

I could make out their words, but nothing held meaning. They floated above the horrific visions I continued to see and wrestle against.

"Why? Give her to me." Michael jogged beside us, rubbing at my hand. His touch burned at the moment and I managed to pull my arm away.

"Because she's consumed the power of the ancients, Michael. She's either going to die from it, or if she's strong enough, she'll consume it and it'll become part of her."

"Making her evil?" Michael paused as Caleb slowed down.

"Making her the greatest weapon known to man or angel. She'll defeat her father, but first she has to defeat this... the battle wasn't in the forest with Malaz. It's here now, in the center of her soul."

My eyelids fluttered closed and I exhaled as the pain inside of me ceased for a minute. I knew how to tame the evil, how to destroy it, but I wasn't sure how to do so while keeping my baby safe. My spirit hovered around my womb, like a scared warrior, desperate to protect the only thing that mattered.

"Help me," I mumbled and reached out. Someone's hand covered mine, the touch no longer burning.

"I'm right here, Rouge. Fight it! Fight it and come back to me. I need you. We need you. Never stop fighting."

I released his hand and tried to nod. He was right. I could do this. I had to.

Chapter 15

I lost all track of time as I struggled to stop the battle raging on inside of me. It could have been minutes, hours, days. I had no idea how long I fought against the dark, and doing everything I could to protect the baby inside of me at the same time. I tossed and turned, thrashing and fighting. Someone would pull me close as I cried out over and over. Then I would push them away as if their touch burned me. Only to cry out again for help.

When I finally felt myself begin to fail from exhaustion, I wrapped my spirit around the child in my womb, curling around to protect it, refusing to let the darkness penetrate through me. I would not let this child suffer or die because of me. The darkness, as if finally understanding my determination and will, stopped its torment.

I have no idea if it left, or simply went dormant but suddenly everything went quiet... peaceful.

Sunlight streaming across my face woke me. The brightness made me wonder if I was trapped in heaven.

I slowly opened my eyes against the glare and realized it was the sun coming through the windows of the cabin, directly on my face. I closed my eyes and then quickly opened them again.

I was alive!

My hands went instinctively around my belly and I swore I felt a flutter of butterflies inside. The baby had survived as well! Had it just been a dream? I knew it hadn't. Something had changed inside of me. I just didn't understand what—yet.

I breathed in deeply and rolled onto my back to stretch my aching body. My eyes closed as my mouth yawned.

Hot breath brushed against my face and I sensed someone close beside me.

I opened my eyes.

Rob.

Maybe an inch from my face. His face scrunched as he stared closely at me.

I swatted him away. "What the hell, Rob?"

"You alive? Is it you?"

I sat up as he stayed on his knees leaning away from me slightly. "Of course it's me!"

He squinted. "Your eyes are blue."

I rolled them, but smiled despite myself. "What color were you hoping for? Rainbow? You sound disappointed."

He raised his hands defensively. "Rainbow would have been cool," he joked and then suddenly lurched forward and wrapped me in a tight hug. "You're alive."

I hugged him back and managed to turn my head away from being buried in his muscular chest. "For now. You might kill me."

"Oops! Yeah, sorry." He let me go.

I sat back, rolling my tired shoulders slowly. "I need something to drink. My throat's dry."

He got up and walked to the door. "Want something to eat too?"

"No, not yet." He started to go, but I stopped him. "Rob?"

"Yeah?" He turned around and leaned against the doorframe lazily.

"Is Michael okay?"

"Right as rain, sister. Right as rain." He grinned and disappeared to go to the kitchen.

I moved to the edge of the bed and tugged my t-shirt up, wanting to check again on the baby.

"Morning, little guy." I rubbed softly, surprised at how much I was showing. It hadn't been but a month or so and yet my stomach was swollen enough to tell. Nothing too exciting, but a subtle shift from the flattened surface I was used to. "You okay in there?"

A knock at the door caught me by surprise and I yanked my shirt down and turned to face Michael as he moved into the room. I stood gingerly, testing my legs, and was relieved to see I was okay. Tired, but alive. I slid into his arms as he wrapped me in a tight hug. He pressed his face to the side of my neck and breathed in deeply.

"You scared the shit out of me." He kissed the soft skin below my ear.

"I'm so sorry. I didn't realize what would happen when I walked back up there. I felt something calling out to me, but honestly..." I pulled back and looked up into his handsome face. "I didn't control anything that happened. It was like something deep down inside of me took over and everything unraveled without my help."

"Crazy. I cannot imagine some of the things you've seen. Some of the things you've been through." He reached up and brushed his fingers through my hair. "I love you. I'm so glad you're okay. I was scared all night."

"Did you stay with me?" I rubbed his sides, trying to offer him comfort. "How long was I... uh, out?"

"One hell of a rough night."

As if on cue, he yawned and I couldn't help but smile. Michael didn't get tired. He'd have fought that battle with one of his arms tied behind his back and not been winded. I slid my fingers through his and squeezed. Even if the darkness lived inside of me now, I had found peace for the moment. Being with Michael would always center me. He helped remind me that I didn't have to worry about what was coming up next, because after it was all said and done, he would be mine and I would be his for the rest of our lives.

I moved back and pulled my hand up between us, staring at my ring and smiling like a kid at Christmas.

"It's too simple, but when we get through all of this—"

I lifted my gaze to him and gave him a warning glare. "I love it and unless it turns my finger green, I'll be wearing it for the rest of my life."

He chuckled. "It's real, just a simple gold band. I'd have liked to get you a big diamond." He shrugged, a goofy boyish grin on his face. "Not many options at the pawnshop."

"It's perfect. I don't need, or want, anything else." I inhaled deeply, about to yawn when I thought I smelled something. I sniffed again. "I smell bacon. Someone cooking?"

"Yeah. Sarah." He dropped to the bed and moved to lie on his back, watching me intently as I stripped out of my clothes and got dressed for the day.

"Like what you see?" I teased him and turned in a slow circle after getting my bra and panties on.

"Are you kidding me? You're the most beautiful woman in the world. Why you're with me, I'll never understand."

"Because we both like graveyards?" I finished getting dressed as he chuckled. Our first meeting was awkward and off the beaten path to say the least. Remembering the early days helped to simplify things often for me.

"You're okay, right?" His voice was soft as concern swept across his face. "Rob came racing out and said you were. I just... I need..." His words trailed off, unsure of how to finish.

"I think I'm okay. I feel good if it's any consolation." I moved to the door and opened it. "I'm hungry. Me and this baby need grub."

He laughed. "I'm going to shower. I stink. Sweat and worry don't make a sexy man."

"You always smell good to me."

"Grace wouldn't agree with you."

I laughed. The feeling felt amazing inside of me. "You shower. Me eat."

Michael raised an eyebrow. "You Tarzan? Me Jane?"

"Something like that." I liked his role reversal joke. "Go shower then, I'll save you a plate." I closed the door and slipped out into the hallway.

Rob and Grace were joking when I walked into the kitchen. The sound of them getting along caused my heart to lighten. A better day was coming. I just needed to cling to the promises of it arriving soon.

"Hey. There's the star of the show." Rob smiled and turned to face me.

"Oh Rouge. I was so worried." Grace crossed the room and pulled me into a tight hug.

Sarah turned from the stove and gave me a smile. "We're so proud of you. You were beyond brave to do what you did."

"Thank you." I returned the smile and hoped our painful past could somehow just be buried along with the promise of a normal life. "Where's Caleb?"

"He's outside chopping wood." She rolled her eyes and turned back to the stove. "Breakfast will be ready in ten minutes."

"Chopping wood?" I mouthed to Grace and turned, walking to the back door and slipping out. I didn't have much to say to him, but I knew he would have questions for me.

The axe sat in a large log, but Caleb wasn't working to split anything from what I could tell. A glimpse of red caught my attention and I spotted him at the edge of the forest, walking around in a circle as if pacing.

I took my time walking up to greet him in hopes of him seeing me and not being surprised by my approach. He wasn't too fond of me, which was his loss, but me making matters worse by spooking him wasn't a desire I had.

"Rouge. You're up." He stopped and slipped his hands into his jean's pockets. "We were worried."

"I'm good." I walked into the forest and moved past him to inspect the beautiful black statue of Malaz. "Incredible."

"I must say that I completely agree." He moved up beside me and glanced down at me. "Thank you."

"For?" I left all emotion out of my voice, deciding it was time to start acting like the woman I was and not the child I wanted to be.

"For taking this dangerous step and proving to all of us... proving to me... that you're on the side of good." He reached out and touched Malaz's arm, brushing his finger over a rosary that ran down the side of his sleeve. "He was once a good man. My brother actually."

"What?" I turned to pin Caleb with a hard stare. "Why didn't you tell us that?"

"Because he died a long time ago when he turned his back on all that was good and harbored darkness." Caleb crossed his arms over his chest, his eyes on Malaz with a sadness in them that I understood.

"And if I wouldn't have killed him, then you would have?" I knew the answer, but I had to ask the question.

"Yes. There is no greater power than love, Rouge, but it's often used as a weapon. I used Michael's love for me and Sarah to get him to come home because I knew he would deliver you and Rob." He let out a painful sigh. "I'm not sorry I did it, but the way in which I went about it left me feeling no better than my brother here. Fighting for the light can lead you into dark places."

I didn't speak because I was truly unsure of what to say. He hadn't apologized, but confirmed his decision to bring harm to me and Rob. It seemed as if nothing had changed.

"And in my desire to destroy you because you felt too powerful, too different from what I believed to be right, true and good... I almost destroyed the only weapon capable of saving us all." He turned to face me. "I'm a product of what I was created to do. I'm laser focused on serving the light and bringing an end to the Grollics. I think by holding tight to that calling, I could ignore the greater one, which was letting my brother move across the earth and spill his disease and pestilence. You've released me from that burden, and for that I can't thank you enough."

I blurted out the first thing that came to mind. A truth that I needed him to know before we moved forward in the fight we were headed toward.

"I'm not killing Bentos until I understand how to do so without killing the innocent Grollics." I lifted my hand as he started to butt in. "Just as there are dark angels, there are innocent, good Grollics. They exist and my brother Rob is one of them. He's been fighting for me diligently, though he has to know that the end is near and will be at my command."

Caleb nodded. "I see your point, though I'm not sure I entirely agree."

"I want your pledge here and now that no matter what happens in this next battle, if I bring Bentos to destruction, that you will leave me be. That you'll never bring death to my door again and my life will become as precious as your own in terms of preservation. Me, Michael, my son, Grace and Rob, should he survive."

Caleb nodded. "I can do that."

"Swear it on Sarah's life that you'll not harm any of us once this is over." I extended my hand.

"I swear it on Sarah's life." He shook my hand.

I turned and walked back to the house without another word. I would take on the mantle of the Grollics because to do so would mean that no one could ever wipe them out in one fatal swipe. My life was protected from that day forth and for that freedom, I would extend it to my father's people and repay them for the death and darkness that he'd so generously spread since his creation.

Rob opened the back door as I moved toward him.

"Everything okay?" He looked past me, narrowing his eyes.

"Yeah. Couldn't be better." I moved into the living room and made my way to the kitchen.

Sarah handed me a plate and reached over, rubbing my back softly. "Breakfast's ready."

"Looks great." I moved up and took a helping and a half of everything. Something told me it was time to get my strength up and food was my number one choice for doing so.

"Is Caleb still out there?" she asked as she lifted a coffee mug to her lips.

"Yeah. We had a short conversation, but it was a good one."

"Can you ever forgive us?" She pursed her lips as if waiting for me to attack her.

"I'm not sure, but I want to try to." I moved to the table and sat down.

She slid into the chair across from me and set her cup down. "I understand that."

"Good." I took a bite of my eggs and groaned. "These are so good."

She chuckled. "They keep me around for a reason. I think it's my eggs."

I looked up to pinpoint where Rob and Grace were, but didn't see them anywhere.

Sarah reached across the table and touched the ring on my finger. "Michael proposed?"

"Yes, and I accepted." I kept my eyes on my plate, not trusting the woman across the table enough to really share with her.

"I'm glad. You're going to make a strong family." She let out a short sigh. "When Michael and Grace lost their family, I took them in. Then I met Caleb and we exchanged Sioghras. We spent hours together trying to decide how to build a home with them. I wanted so badly to turn their heartbreak into love and our motley crew into a true family."

I glanced up, not able to keep my emotions on lock down. "And you did."

"Yes. We worked hard at it though." Her eyes filled with tears as she watched me. "It's funny how thinking you know best can quickly turn against you. I never would have hurt either of them in a million years."

"Everyone makes mistakes, Sarah." I pressed my hand to my throat and brushed my fingers over my chest, making sure my Sioghra was still in place. It was, but for some odd reason it was heavier than usual.

"I know, but we've made a grave one. I'm praying we can resurrect what we destroyed." She reached up and wiped her tears away before forcing a smile. "I've realized one thing that I think will stay with me forever."

"What's that?" I leaned back, forcing myself to focus on the beautiful woman across from me.

"Evil is bred, not born." She sniffled and turned as the back door opened.

Caleb walked in and stopped behind her, sliding his hands onto her shoulders and leaning over to kiss the top of her head. "Everything okay?"

"Yeah... it will be," I responded and picked up a piece of bacon. "I didn't realize you guys were holding out on us. Sarah's a great cook."

"Yep. I had to have some reason to keep her around." Caleb winked at me and for the first time since meeting him, I felt as if there might be room for a relationship between the two of us. Not a close one, but something other than the two of us being at each other's throats with pitchforks.

"See... I told you it was my cooking." She laughed and I smiled, grateful that I didn't have to force it.

The day was young and there was a lot of planning left to do. Michael needed to rest and then I would drag him with me into the backyard. We could plan out where everyone was going to be and what their involvement would look like when I called my father from wherever he was.

Knowing him, he wasn't far at all.

The thought alone scared me to the center of my soul. Malaz hadn't been a hard defeat at all until his essence mixed with mine, then the battle began. Bentos would be a different story altogether. He was already part of me, so there would be no joining. The battle was set to be external, his strength and power against mine.

I needed to figure out how to unlock the strength of three and fast. The journal said that having Malaz defeated and indwelt inside of me would trigger the greatest weapon of all time. I just needed to unlock what the weapon was and how to wield it.

Chapter 16

Michael sat with me as I pored over the journals, tossing each one on the floor as I found nothing to help us. Frustrated, I tossed the last one on top of the others and reached out to tug Michael toward me, wrapping my arms around him and kissing him a few times on the side of the head before he playfully swatted me away.

Things had changed so incredibly much over the last year of our journey. The stiff, proper boy I'd fallen in love with was still very much that same boy, and yet different. It was as if the pregnancy changed him, softened him just a little where I was concerned.

"What are you two up to?" Grace asked as she walked into the room.

"We were just talking about the strength of three." Michael laughed, pointed to himself, me and then the baby in my belly.

Grace sat down and shook her head. "You really think that's the secret?"

I shook my head and sat up, forcing Michael to sit as well. "I'm trying to figure out what happened yesterday and how I'm going to harness this supposedly hidden power inside of me."

Grace nodded. "Seems like the dark angel's power was part of what Rouge needed to unlock the strength, but now we're still at a loss."

"I'm not so sure it's not me, the baby and you." I glanced over at him, still grasping at straws, because in all actuality, nothing made sense. There were too many of us to group some of us in the scenario and not others. However, Michael's joking around kind of did make sense.

"What if it's twins?" Michael smirked and it was my turn to swat at him.

"Ha-ha. You're a funny man, Michael." I poked him in the ribs and then stopped when Grace cleared her throat impatiently.

"Maybe it's not three people. Maybe it's three things inside of someone that make them the weapon all by themselves?" Grace offered.

The door opened and Rob walked in, taking a seat on the arm of Grace's chair. She reached up and scratched at his back as he closed his eyes and pushed against her touch.

It was nice to know that if something happened to me, Grace would love my brother.

"Where have you been?" I asked my brother.

"Outside talking to Sarah. She's really a nice lady. Throws a great hook, but still a nice lady." He gave me a goofy grin.

"Did she hit you?" I stiffened at the thought.

"No. She was working out by the outhouse. Guess she found a punching bag. We were just talking about the upcoming fight. She had a good idea, but I'm not sure if I'm down with trying it." He shrugged and adverted his gaze toward the ground.

"What was the idea?" Michael moved closer to me and reached out, taking my hand.

"That I should call Joshua's old pack to my side and invoke alpha rights." He looked up and focused on me. "Not sure I get the point of all that though. I'd have no rights at all once dad showed up."

I bit on my lip, thinking through the situation. It would be nice to have Rob as the leader of a group of Grollics that could join our side of the fray, but he was right. If Bentos wanted to take control of them, he could. Unless...

"Do you remember back at the beach in Florida when we had that huge fight with Bentos?" I released Michael's hand and moved up to the edge of my seat.

"Um, yeah. How could we forget?" Grace laughed and got an eye roll from me for her efforts.

"Bentos didn't take control of the Grollics that were under my control. Remember that?"

"I do." Michael moved to the edge of the couch too before standing. "Do you think it was because you took control of Joshua? You made him subordinate to you?"

"I don't know, but whatever we did... it worked, right?"

Rob stood and ran his fingers through his hair. "Yes. It did."

"So let Rouge take ownership of you and then call the wolves to you and take ownership of them." Grace reached up and tugged at his hand.

"You think that would work?" He turned his attention to me while grasping onto Grace's extended hand.

"I think it's damn well worth a try. We need more fighters on our side. If I know Bentos, I know without a doubt that he'll be bringing everything he has at his disposal." I shrugged and moved closer to Michael.

"Especially since he knows that Caleb and Sarah are here with us." Michael pulled me into a quick hug and released me, heading toward the back door. "Speaking of... I need to see if they're willing to call the remaining hunters to join us. When and where is this battle going to happen?"

"Tonight. Here." I forced a calm facade in place as the room exploded with concerns and questions.

Everyone had an opinion, but the truth was that it was time. Inside me, I had no doubt at all that it was time to end the war. The strength of three would be revealed to me. I just knew it. I needed to find a few minutes that I could spend by myself with my journal in solitude.

"This isn't open for discussion. I'm following my instincts. You can back me up, or pack up. I'm tired of running and losing. Tonight's our night. I'm more than sure of it." I lifted my hands to get everyone's attention as I spoke over them. "Stop bitching and get up. Let's get busy doing everything we can to prepare. It's happening tonight."

Michael nodded and walked from the house.

Rob let out a long sigh and glanced down at Grace. "I'm going to go call the other Grollics in the area. You wanna come or do you need to do something too?"

"I'll come with you." She got up and glanced over her shoulder at me with a weary look on her pretty face. "You haven't even figured out how to save Rob."

"I will. I promise."

The doubt in her eyes hurt me, but I knew where she was coming from. She had fallen in love with my brother. If it was Michael whose life was on the line, I would be fighting tooth and nail to keep everything constant until we were assured that he would be with us forever.

I walked back down the hall to the bedroom and pulled out my journal, making a pact to myself that I wouldn't call on Bentos until everyone was in position and I understood my part. Turning back down the hall, I walked to the front door as I held the warming journal to my chest.

A glimmer of light caught my attention as it fluttered above the dark lake just a few feet from the front door. It almost looked like a firefly, but those never came out during the day. I walked toward the water and squinted as the small insect danced along the top of the water and moved downstream.

Untying the boat, I got in and ignored the fear that tried to permeate my soul over the waters below me. I shoved off the dock hard and sat down, trying to keep my balance so that the boat wouldn't flip.

The paddles on the floor of the canoe would help me steer, but I had no clue where I was going, so it seemed a waste of physical energy.

My Sioghra warmed against my chest and I tugged it out, both mine and Michael's laying in my hand. His was unchanged, the brilliant garnet red blood sparkling as it moved around in its casing. Mine was dark as midnight and the shimmery essence of goodness in it made the liquid look like the stars in the sky might.

I brushed my finger over the top of mine and let out a long sigh. The dark angel was part of me, but what did that really mean? Was I in danger of becoming something evil like he was? I was already fighting against my father's blood flowing through my veins. Now this?

The firefly fluttered before me, its little wings making the sound of a thousand violins as it passed me.

I picked up the oar beside me and paddled hard to force the boat to a rickety dock that sat to my left. The bug had gone that way, and where some part of me knew I was being silly, the other parts knew that nothing was to be left up to chance anymore.

After tying the boat to the dock, I leapt out onto the rotting wood and jogged up the path that led to an opening in the forest. The weather was chilly and I found myself wishing I'd put on a jacket. My t-shirt and jeans weren't doing much to keep me warm. A shiver ran through me and I slipped the journal under my shirt, pressing it to the skin of my chest for warmth.

"Rouge." The feminine voice was soft and too ethereal to figure out who it was.

I jerked around to find my mother standing in front of me again. "Mom?"

She smiled in a way that let me know my response to her meant something.

"I'm sorry about yesterday. I can't be in the presence of evil in this form."

Her dress was white and large white wings fluttered frantically behind her. I glanced down and noticed her feet hovered just above the ground. Peace radiated from her and I found myself wanting to draw nearer, but something told me that it would be inappropriate.

"What can we do to get you into heaven?" I pulled the journal out and laid it at my feet. "Surely there's something we can do, right?"

"I've been granted ascension because of my sacrifice for you and Rob. It will happen sometime soon. I've come to say goodbye and to give you a gift." She smiled as tears filled her pretty sapphire eyes.

"Oh thank goodness." I let out the breath I'd been holding. "I don't want you to go, but knowing that you're going to make it into heaven... that means everything."

Her smile was kind and the air around her warm as she moved to stand in front of me.

"What you did yesterday was so brave." She reached out and touched my face, warming me to the center of my soul. "I love you and Rob so much. Tell him for me?"

"Of course." I tried to hold back my tears, but with my vision blurring quickly, I knew it was no use.

She moved her hand down to my Sioghra and picked it up as a smile slipped over her lips. Tears dripped slowly down her cheeks as she smiled, giving up a soft chuckle as she examined the trinket.

"Incredible." She looked up at me and I swear I'd never seen a more beautiful woman before. "The power of three is you, Rouge. Just you."

"What?" Shock raced through me, quickly followed by terror.

"All of the players in our story have found a stage inside of you." She released the Sioghra and stepped back. "Your father made you a Grollic. I made you a hunter, and Malaz made you a dark angel. We are the key elements in this play that has swept humanity away for all of time. Now we all reside within you in some way or another."

"Me? I don't want it to be me." I shook my head and reached for her.

"But it is, and I believe that you already knew that." She pressed her palm to my chest and ran her hand over my cheek as tears began to drip faster down her pale face. "Everything you need to win this war is inside of you."

"And what about saving Rob?" My voice was tight and gave credence to the hysteria bubbling up inside of me.

"When the time comes, you'll know what to do. Don't hesitate. Rob and every other Grollic will survive this. I have every confidence in you. You should too." She leaned down and kissed my cheek, the sensation like the fluttering of butterfly wings against my face.

"Don't go. I'm scared." I let out a soft sob, but she simply smiled and moved back toward the forest.

"I love you. Be who you were made to be just one more time and then... rest." She faded from my vision and the soft exhale of a woman filled the air around me. Her essence lifted to the sky and I dropped to my knees, alone. Confused. Scared.

"There you are." Michael walked toward me with a huge smile on his face, which was quite out of place for what we had coming our way soon.

"What's going on?" I reached for him, pulling him to me and tucking my face against his chest. I breathed in deeply and worked to find my centering.

"I have a surprise for you, but first, what's wrong?" He moved back and slipped his strong hands around my face, forcing me to look up at him. "Have you been crying?"

"I watched my mother ascend. That was her Sioghra in the stuff we found. The empty one." I closed my eyes and took a shaky breath, trying hard not to lose myself again.

"Wow, but you saw her ascend? How?" His thumbs brushed rhythmically over my cheeks, the sensation soothing.

"Her sacrifice for me and Rob gave her entrance to heaven." I opened my eyes and took a deep breath. "All of the pieces of the puzzle are falling into place."

"Agreed. Let me show you what we've been up to. We got everything together for later tonight, but I want you to relax and come with me for the next little bit."

"Okay." I slipped my hand into his as we walked around the house and toward the dense forest that surrounded the back half of the property. "Did Caleb get a hold of any other hunters?"

"Yes. They will be here by nightfall, or those that can make it in time will. Most of them are hopping on jets and planes as we speak."

I turned to look up at him as we continued to walk. "That's great news."

"Agreed, and Rob said that the Grollics should start piling in any minute." He squeezed my hand. "You need to claim lordship over him when I'm done with you."

"I can do that." I turned and narrowed my eyes as various colors danced just beyond the tree line. "Michael, what's going on?"

"You'll see." His smile was radiant and I honestly didn't care what we were up to. To see that kind of joy and excitement on his handsome face was worth any slight detour from the day.

We walked up to the opening of the forest and my breath caught in my chest. I jolted to a standstill and Michael released me, jogging toward a beautiful display of white flowers and candles that hung from the trees. Caleb stood at the end of the path with a book in his hands, Grace beside him and Sara on the other side. Michael took his place beside Grace as Rob walked toward me with his eyebrow raised.

"You couldn't tell your only brother that you were getting married?"

I balked and slipped my arm into Rob's. "I didn't know I was."

"What? He said he asked you." Rob moved us down the path toward Michael as overwhelming joy and anxiety tore up the center of my chest.

"He did, but I didn't think it would be this fast." I stilled my thoughts and focused on Michael, realizing why he was forcing this to go so quickly. He wanted us together now in case something happened later that night. I was grateful for his decision. It would be the strengthening chord between us and perhaps the saving grace should one of us fall in the battle.

I blinked past my tears and stopped beside my love, my heart.

Rob handed me over, but squeezed in a quick hug while whispering that he loved me.

I choked on a sob and nodded. "I love you too. So much."

"My turn." Michael tugged at me and I laughed, turning to him as Caleb worked through the marriage ceremony.

I repeated my vows as I stared into the beautiful eyes of the boy who had so quickly become a man. Bentos could take away my freedom, my choices, my life, but he would never take away love. It rested deep in the center of me and soon it would be born to a peaceful existence that Michael and I were about to create.

"You're mine. Forever, Rouge. Got it?" He leaned in as his lip lifted in a cocky smirk.

"I would have it no other way." I lifted to my toes, meeting him halfway as he sealed our vows with a kiss. I was his wife now, but a time for celebrating would be later.

Chapter 17

"They're here." Caleb turned from looking out the front door to Sarah. "Come with me to greet them and fill them in on the situation we face."

"Of course." She stood and left with him.

The rest of us sat at the kitchen table in stony silence. Michael played with the ring around my finger, his face solemn and expression saddened.

"I'm terrified." Grace was the first to admit what the darkness between us was.

"Me too." I pulled from Michael's grasp on my hand and brushed my fingers over her arm.

After the ceremony I'd taken Rob's pledge of allegiance. I was his Alpha and the other Grollics would be arriving soon to become his. If a fight was in order to take that role, he was ready to fight. We figured after explaining the battle to come with Bentos that most of them would gladly file in behind us. Everyone was weary from being the bastard's puppet. It was time to right the situation and then release all of them to freedom.

"I'm not." Rob shrugged. "I trust you. If you say that you're ready, then you are."

"I thought I was in times past too." I let out a painful sigh and sat back in my chair. "I pray this time is different."

"It is." Michael brushed my hair off my shoulder. "I can feel it."

A series of howls resounded in the backyard and we all jumped up, Rob jogging for the door and bolting out to greet the

Grollics. I stopped just outside the door and pulled Michael and Grace to stay back with me.

A behemoth of a man walked toward us, his expression angry and eyes menacing. "How dare you call us back to this place? I should kill you for your disrespect of our kind."

"We fight tonight for freedom." Rob spoke with authority like I'd never heard. Some part of me wanted to take a knee and pledge him my allegiance. "Bentos is headed this way soon and we are few in numbers, but mighty in power. Stand with us and I promise you that those of you who survive will walk away free."

"Is she the one?" He nodded toward me, his expression softening slightly.

"I am." I left the comfort of my friends and walked toward the group of men and women gathering behind our guests. "I'm the seventh daughter of the seventh son. Tonight this ends. Join us?"

I lifted my hands and let darkness pour out of me to put the power inside of me on display. I wasn't showing off, but giving validation to my abilities. A large ominous cloud danced above us, its movement sporadic and angry, like a swarm of bees that had quickly gotten out of control. I pulled it back toward me, taking a hard hit to the chest as it permeated my skin and sunk down from wherever it came.

I wanted to scream out at the biting pain of it reentering me, but I refused. They needed to see a solidified hero and they would.

"Rouge!" Michael ran toward me, jerking me around and checking my face for signs of struggle.

"I'm fine. I told you that I was ready." I touched the side of his face. "I am."

"We'll give our allegiance to her," the man barked.

I turned on him and shook my head. "No. You'll give it to my brother. My life is likely to be extinguished as I alone will fight my father. Your best bet is to be protected under the covering of my brother. I'll not take no for an answer."

The male nodded, as did many others behind him. Rob moved forward and started the work of the Grollics, taking under his wing more than two hundred willing and capable beasts.

My father would bring far more, but where he had puppets, we had captives who were tired of their chains. Men would fight for many things, but freedom was at the top of the list.

"Tonight we bring closure to this war." I walked back into the house and picked up my journal. It was time.

It was as if heaven knew that we were facing hell that night. The darkened sky was covered in dense grey clouds, leaving the feeling of despair in the air around us. I stood in the middle of the large field behind the cabin. A calm sat on me like I'd never felt before, but the loss of emotion worried me.

I glanced behind me and looked at the faces of my family, my friends and my enemies.

"Ready?" I asked.

"Yes, and know that I'm with you completely." Michael lifted his fingers to his lips and blew me a kiss.

"As am I." Rob's voice was deep and commanding.

"And me," Grace added at the same time as Sarah.

"And me as well. I'm right behind you should you need my strength or a rest in the fight." Caleb lifted his chin as he spoke and I forced tears back.

The voices that lifted around me, confirming that I was covered by a multitude of fighters, both hunters and Grollics who stood side by side, united for the first and possibly last time in human history.

I nodded and closed my eyes, letting the incantation roll off of my tongue.

"From the north and south bring the power of three.
As you rise from the valley, come and stand before me.

Try and take what is mine as the world becomes dark,
For the father shall die and awake the seventh mark."

The wind blew hard against me and a deep laugh filled the air, my father more than joyful at having another opportunity to stand before his enemies and reign supreme no doubt.

Not tonight, asshole.

He walked toward me with his head held high. Beautiful wouldn't begin to describe him, but evil always needed the most alluring of covers... it's how they got you. His dark copper hair blew in the wind as it played along the side of his alabaster face. His eyes were amber and lit up as if small fireflies danced behind his gaze, but it was his expression that drove a stake of fear down inside of me.

He was willing to do anything necessary to survive.

Good thing I was too.

"Have you come to put an end to this madness?" He smiled at me and lifted his hands as the forests shook violently.

I kept my facade in place and nodded. "I have. Your time is over, much like Malaz has met his end."

He flinched subtly. "Lies. You speak lies, child. I'm almost proud."

I refused to defend myself to him. "You've raped, pillaged and killed for far too long in the name of greed and power. Tonight you end... forever."

"Come, daughter. Let us dance."

I scoffed, nearly laughing out loud at his choice of words. I'd just married Michael and this was going to be the father-daughter dance?

Bentos lifted his foot and slammed it on the ground, shaking the earth and jolting everyone behind us but me.

The forests split open and hundreds of Grollics in beast form poured out of the trees. I charged at my father, knowing that Rob would instruct our warriors what to do and that Caleb would keep his hunters on the right side of the line.

My job was to kill Bentos and take back the life source for our people. It was my only focus. It had to be.

He spun, leaving me jolting past him before turning on my heel and releasing the darkness inside of me.

A smile touched his mouth as he opened wide and swallowed the essence that I forced toward him. He licked his lips and rubbed his stomach. "More, please."

"What the hell?" I growled and lifted my hands, subverting his punches and kicks as we spun around the fighting that surrounded us.

"It's not that easy, child. You should have known this, and you would have, if you would have accepted my invitation to join me." He jerked around me and caught me, pulling me violently against his body and trapping me in a chokehold. A knife pressed to my throat and he laughed, pressing his lips to my ear.

"This seems familiar. No second chances from your mother this time though. Too bad. You were promising."

I pressed against his arm, grateful that he'd done exactly what I needed him to. It was the essence of life that had taken Malaz's life and it would be the same that would take my father's. Grabbing my Sioghra I tugged it free from my neck and turned, snapping it open and dousing him with the dark contents inside of it.

"No!!!" he wailed. "What have you done, Jamie? You insolent little bitch! No!!!!" He reached for me, but the dark cloud started at his feet and rushed up far more quickly than it had Malaz. His eyes turned dark as night and he lifted a hand as the spell began to turn his legs into onyx. "Make it stop or I'll kill him. I will. Test me in this."

I turned to see Rob dangling from the air, his eyes wide as oxygen was rushing from his body.

"Stop! Leave him be! Stop it!" I lurched toward my father and plowed into him, tugging at his arm as I screamed in his face.

"You make it stop," he screamed back. His voice grated across my face and I swore I was bleeding from a thousand tiny cuts.

The darkness continued to rise up to his midsection and Rob cried out loudly as he was jerked around in mid-air.

"Leave him alone, damn you!" I released more darkness from my hands, forcing it to coat my father faster. If I could kill him before Rob ran out of air...

A laugh left Bentos and he shook his head. "The master is always greater than the servant, Rouge. This isn't over."

A sickening crack resounded behind me. I turned in time to watch my brother fall from the sky, his neck broken and body lifeless on the ground.

The scream that ripped out of the center of me shook the ground beneath us and caused everything to stop. I dropped to my knees as the last bit of my father's face was consumed by the dark wind. It leapt into the air and danced like a whirlwind for a few more minutes before rushing toward me and wrapping me up tightly in its hold.

As it spun faster and faster, it began to suck the oxygen from my lungs. Dizziness raced over me and I could hear the distant screams of my friends for someone to do something, but there was nothing they could do.

My mother said I would know the point at which I could take the Grollics' life source into myself. This was it. I had the power to reject my father's blood mingling with mine, but to do so would kill everyone that Rob fought beside. He believed in them and I did too. I couldn't let his sacrifice be for nothing.

I relaxed and air filled my lungs as the darkness dove into my Sioghra, the pain of it numbing me. Pressing my hands to the earth, I gasped for air over and over until the violence ended.

I dropped to the earth, my cheek hitting the cold ground as life came crashing down. My mother and brother were dead, and inside of me lay the darkness of the world. How could I get up and live after what I'd seen? After what I'd done?

Tears rolled over my nose and puddled on the ground below me as I stared blankly at the statue of my father.

Strong arms picked me up, but I couldn't begin to comprehend anything that moment.

All I could hear were Grace's horrified screams over Rob's lifeless body.

They were in harmony to mine.

Epilogue

7 months later

The ocean breeze felt good against my skin as I stood at the edge of our beach house, the scene before me a great reminder as to why we did all that we had done. To preserve life in the midst of darkness was a lie. We needed freedom and room to move around without threat.

"You doing okay?" Michael moved up behind me and wrapped his arms around me.

I nodded, but flinched as a pain ripped through my abdomen. "I think so."

"Are you in pain?" He moved around to look down into my face. His open white shirt and jeans looked perfect on him and I couldn't help but take a minute to enjoy the best view in the world.

"Just a contraction." I reached out and flinched again. "They're getting closer and closer."

"I'll call Maria." Michael pulled me close and kissed the side of my face. "Go into the house and lay down on the couch."

"Okay." I walked in behind him as he pulled out his phone and called the closest mid-wife to us.

After all we'd been through, we decided to part ways with most of our family and buy a small beach house where we planned to grow old together. It was peaceful and filled with love and laughter, which is all I ever wanted anyway.

I made it to the couch as another contraction hit and my water broke. I leaned back, not caring about the mess, but only about the safe arrival of our son. I assumed it was a boy from the incredible amount of jabbing and kicking I got over the last four to five months. I couldn't go to a doctor to confirm, but after everything and the strength of my body, I knew he and I would make it through the birthing just fine.

"Michael! He's coming, I think," I cried out and tried to control my breathing as my sweet husband raced back into the room and stopped short.

"Oh man..." He shook his head and moved toward me, sitting down and reaching out to brush my hair back.

"You don't have to be in here to see this. Call Grace. She can help me." I closed my eyes and cried out as another contraction ripped through me.

"Okay. Yeah. I'll call Grace. Hold on." He got up and ran from the room, getting a chuckle out of me.

The man could slaughter a pack of wolves and roll around in their blood, but watching his wife give birth was too much.

It seemed like forever before he returned to the living room, but both Maria and Grace were with him. They rushed into action, getting warm water and towels, and barking at Michael to do various chores just to keep him busy as the time came for me to push.

"I'm scared." I reached out and took Grace's hand as tears filled her beautiful blue eyes.

"There's no reason to be. We're right here. All of us are." She squeezed my hand and moved to the side as Maria got in my face.

The elderly mid-wife had been a godsend and was forceful in her commands, but gentle with her touch. She pressed on my knees and smiled. "Time to push. Give me a good one."

All that we'd been through over the last year raced through my mind, my memories giving me a picture show of sorts as I forced my body to do what was natural to it.

The trials and tribulations that Michael and I had been through were more than most would survive or recover from, and yet here we were... starting a family together.

"It's a boy! A beautiful, healthy boy!" Maria cried out and worked with Grace to wrap up the baby. "Wait... push again, Rouge."

I did, not quite lucid enough to understand anything other than the woman's demanding voice. The afterbirth needed to come out. I'd read that sometimes it can be more painful than the birth of the child. I pushed hard and lifted my chin to the ceiling as pain ripped through me.

"There's another baby, child."

"Pardon? What?" I lifted my head, unable to comprehend.

"Twins." She grinned at me. "You did not know?"

She focused as a contraction ripped through me, cutting any response from me off.

"Push again, Rouge," she commanded and worked with me to get the other baby out of my womb.

I collapsed as tears filled my eyes. *Twins?*

"This one is a girl," Maria smiled and then spoke to the man standing by my head, the one who hadn't whispered a word while I pushed his children out. "Michael... come bring your children to your wife."

Michael moved closer to me, leaning down near my head and kissed me over and over as he laughed through tears. "We have two! A boy and a girl."

I smiled and closed my eyes for a moment, fighting the exhaustion. "You're on diaper duty this week."

"I'm so proud of you." He kissed me again and moved to take both of the babies before settling beside me and presenting them.

I turned and smiled before leaning over and pressing a kiss to each of their little heads. "They look like you and Grace with that mop of blond hair."

Maria covered me up and stood, smiling toward the back door as she called out, "It's safe. Come on in."

I shifted the babies in my arms to show them off.

"I think they look like me, which is a treat and a half." My brother moved up beside Michael and wrapped an arm around his shoulder as he smiled. "Good job, Mikey. Twins?"

I still hadn't gotten used to Rob's bright blue eyes, or the Sioghra around his neck, but I was beyond grateful for it. We had thought we'd lost him the night we had stopped Bentos, but he'd surprised us all after the battle when he'd rolled over and stood, his piercing blue eyes rising like a beacon in the night. Then, in typical Rob fashion, he'd started dancing and singing 'Thriller' by Michael Jackson. I could have killed him—again.

He made silly baby noises now to his new niece and nephew. "What do you think Grace?" He straightened and hugged his wife. They'd gotten married a few months back here at the beach. "Time for us to start practicing. You know, try and make one of these ourselves?"

I rolled my eyes and laughed as Michael growled at his brother-in-law.

"Easy, mate," Rob teased. "Not in the front of the kids."

"Same goes," Michael warned, but the twitching of his lips gave way to laughter. He lifted our daughter off my right arm and handed her to Grace and then handed Rob our son.

I let Maria help to reposition me and clear the room.

"Names. These babies need names!" Rob carefully handed me the baby back and Grace did the same.

Leaning down, I breathed in deeply, taking in the new life I was offered and exhaling the old. "Rebekah?"

"Perfect," Michael murmured as he leaned down close to the three of us. He rubbed his nose gently over Rebekah's forehead. "Hello 'Becka. Welcome to our crazy world."

Now our son. He needed a strong name, one to break all the tradition of the seventh mark.

Michael looked up at me, as if reading my thoughts. "Jamie? Rob still calls you it half the time, what about Jamie?" He nodded back at my brother. "He'll probably call him Rouge, but still..."

"Jamie." I looked down at our son, his head turning as if he'd heard his name. "A new story for Rebekah and Jamie."

"I love you," Michael whispered and bent down, pressing a soft kiss on my lips.

"I love all of you." I blinked past my tears. "I never thought I'd have a real family."

Michael leaned in and brushed his lips by the twins' heads. "Me most, right?"

"You most... forever."

After all the pain and scars of destruction had washed away, two new heartbeats fluttered against my chest. Would these children have a better life than we had? Would darkness lurk in the shadows, ready to bite? They were hybrids, angel blood and Grollic blood running through them.

What would their future hold?

THE END

Dear Hidden Secrets Saga Fans!

Thanks for reading and sticking with me through each book in the series!

I felt this was a clean spot to end, with an HEA (not sure what HEA is, message me on FB or my website, or google the term. I had to the first time too *wink wink*), but the story also the potential to continue.

This is where you come in! I'd love to hear if readers still want more. Or if you're content, that works for me too!

You're always welcome to join me on new adventures and as often as I can, I put my first books free so you can test the waters!

Happy Reading!

W.J. May

The Hidden Secrets Saga:

Book Trailer: http://www.youtube.com/watch?v=Y-_vVYC1gvo
Download Seventh Mark part 1 For FREE
Seventh Mark part 2
Marked by Destiny
Compelled
Fate's Intervention
Chosen Three

FIND W.J. May

Website: http://www.wanitamay.yolasite.com

Facebook:
https://www.facebook.com/pages/Author-WJ-May-FAN-PAGE

Newsletter:

SIGN UP FOR W.J. May's Newsletter to find out about new releases, updates, cover reveals and even freebies!

http://eepurl.com/97aYf

Books by W.J. May

The X Files Series:
Code X – Coming January 2016
Book 1

Seventeen-year-old Whitney Monroe is a child of untapped potential whose only outlet into the world is through her computer and the cybernetic wilderness that she has limitless access to. Better than most hackers, Whitney engages in cyber-vigilantism, but also knows that she's more than a little drawn to uncovering secrets. Eventually she's going to get caught, but how many dark and mysterious sites can she stop before she does?

Rae of Hope
The Chronicles of Kerrigan

The Chronicles of Kerrigan
Book I - *Rae of Hope* **is FREE!**
Book Trailer: http://www.youtube.com/watch?v=gILAwXxx8MU

Hidden Secrets Saga:
Download Seventh Mark part 1 For FREE
Book Trailer:
http://www.youtube.com/watch?v=Y-_vVYC1gvo

Book Blurb:

Like most teenagers, Rouge is trying to figure out who she is and what she wants to be. With little knowledge about her past, she has questions but has never tried to find the answers. Everything changes when she befriends a strangely intoxicating family. Siblings Grace and Michael, appear to have secrets which seem connected to Rouge. Her hunch is confirmed when a horrible incident occurs at an outdoor party. Rouge may be the only one who can find the answer.

An ancient journal, a Sioghra necklace and a special mark force life-altering decisions for a girl who grew up unprepared to fight for her life or others.

All secrets have a cost and Rouge's determination to find the truth can only lead to trouble...or something even more sinister.

Shadow of Doubt
Part 1 is FREE!

Book Trailer: http://www.youtube.com/watch?v=LZK09Fe7kgA

<u>Book Blurb:</u>

What happens when you fall for the one you are forbidden to love?

Erebus is a bit of a lost soul. He's a guy so he should be out to have fun but unlike the rest of his kind, he is solemn and withdrawn. That is, until he meets Aurora, a law student at Cornell University. His entire world is shaken. Feelings he's never had and urges he's never understood take over. These strange longings drive him to question everything about himself

When a jealous ex stalks back into his life, he must decide if he is willing to risk everything to be with Aurora. His desire for her could destroy her, or worse, erase his own existence forever.

Courage Runs Red
The Blood Red Series
Book 1 is FREE

Book Blurb:

What if courage was your only option?

When Kallie lands a college interview with the city's new hot-shot police officer, she has no idea everything in her life is about to change. The detective is young, handsome and seems to have an unnatural ability to stop the increasing local crime rate. Detective Liam's particular interest in Kallie sends her heart and head stumbling over each other.

When a raging blood feud between vampires spills into her home, Kallie gets caught in the middle. Torn between love and family loyalty she must find the courage to fight what she fears the most and possibly risk everything, even if it means dying for those she loves.

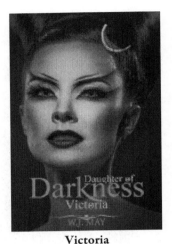

Victoria
FREE!!
Only Death Could Stop Her Now

The Daughters of Darkness is a series of female heroines who may or may not know each other, but all have the same father, Vlad Montour.

Victoria is a Hunter Vampire, one of the last of her kind. She's the best of the best.

When she finds out one of her marks is actually her sister she let's her go, only to end up on the wrong side of the council.

Forced to prove herself she hunts her next mark, a werewolf. Injured and hungry, she is forced to do what she must to survive. Her actions upset the ancient council and she finds herself now being the one thing she has always despised—the Hunted.

Coming Soon:

The future is not a safe place. When Tay Maslov was a girl, she lived in New York State, and her playground were the sun-drenched fields of her parent's farm. But all that changed when one day the Servitors came, looking for new recruits for their master, the Archon Jeremiah of Brooklyn.

The vampires – or Elders – rule the cities now, and hardly any humans are left out in the wildernesses. All of that land is given over to the weird animal-like Shifters. The Elders run the Blood Banks, enforced Blood Donations, as well as the Blood Clubs, and the culls of insurgents. When Tay Maslov, many years later and now a vampire herself, servant to her Archon Jeremiah, refuses to go on a cull of the poor humans she is cast down, become a Feral; hated by all. It is in this state that she meets Kaiden, himself a creature of the night – but far different from her. Which of them will survive what comes next.

Free Books:

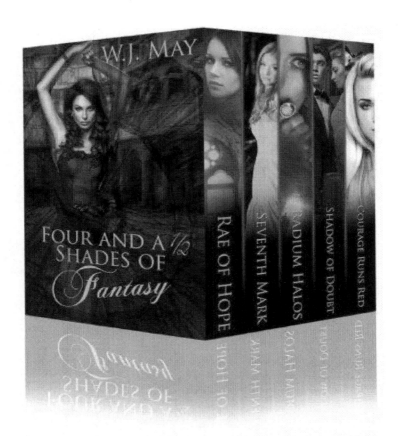

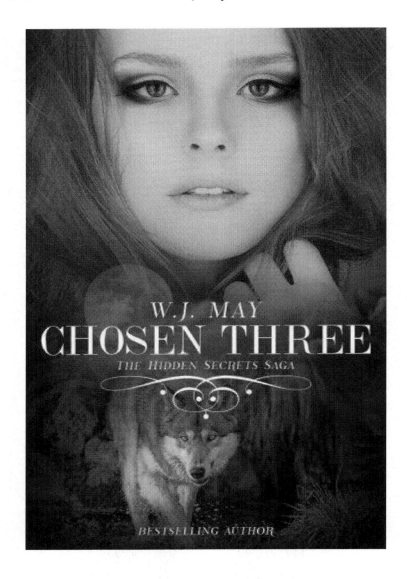

Don't miss out!

Click the button below and you can sign up to receive emails whenever W.J. May publishes a new book. There's no charge and no obligation.

Sign Me Up!

http://books2read.com/r/B-A-SSF-IHQH

BOOKS 2 READ

Connecting independent readers to independent writers.

Did you love *Chosen Three*? Then you should read *Lost Vampire* by W.J. May!

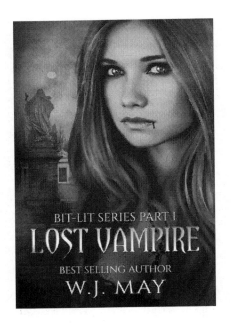

From Bestselling Fantasy/Paranormal author, W.J. May comes a new kind of vampire shifter series. Get ready to be blown away!

Lost Vampire - Book 1 of the Bit-Lit Series

The future is not a safe place.

When Tay Maslov was a girl, she lived in New York State, and her playground were the sun-drenched fields of her parent's farm. But all that changed when one day the Servitors came, looking for new recruits for their master, the Archon Jeremiah of Brooklyn.

The vampires – or Elders – rule the cities now, and hardly any humans are left out in the wildernesses. All of that land is given over to the weird animal-like Shifters. The Elders run the Blood Banks, enforced Blood Donations, as well as the Blood Clubs, and the culls of insurgents.

When Tay Maslov, many years later and now a vampire herself, servant to her Archon Jeremiah, refuses to go on a cull of the poor humans she is cast down, becomes a Feral; hated by all. It is in this state that she meets Kaiden, himself a creature of the night – but far different from her. Which of them will survive what comes next?

Book 1 - Lost Vampire
Book 2 - Cost of Blood
Book 3 - - Coming in January 2016

Also by W.J. May

Bit-Lit Series
Lost Vampire
Cost of Blood
Price of Death

Blood Red Series
Courage Runs Red
The Night Watch
Marked by Courage
Forever Night

Daughters of Darkness: Victoria's Journey
Victoria
Huntress
Coveted (A Vampire & Paranormal Romance)
Twisted

Hidden Secrets Saga
Seventh Mark - Part 1
Seventh Mark - Part 2
Marked By Destiny
Compelled
Fate's Intervention
Chosen Three

The Chronicles of Kerrigan
Rae of Hope
Dark Nebula
House of Cards

Royal Tea
Under Fire
End in Sight
Hidden Darkness
Twisted Together
Mark of Fate
Strength & Power
Last One Standing
Rae of Light

The Chronicles of Kerrigan Prequel
Christmas Before the Magic
Question the Darkness
Into the Darkness

The Hidden Secrets Saga
Seventh Mark (part 1 & 2)

The Senseless Series
Radium Halos
Radium Halos - Part 2
Nonsense

The X Files
Code X
Replica X

Standalone
Shadow of Doubt (Part 1 & 2)
Five Shades of Fantasy
Glow - A Young Adult Fantasy Sampler
Shadow of Doubt - Part 2
Four and a Half Shades of Fantasy
Full Moon

Dream Fighter
What Creeps in the Night
Forest of the Forbidden
HuNted
Arcane Forest: A Fantasy Anthology
Ancient Blood of the Vampire and Werewolf

Made in the USA
San Bernardino, CA
17 March 2017